'You're wrong for each other.'

'How would you know?' Rosalyn asked. 'You know nothing about me.'

'Come here,' he said. She stood, still and frozen. 'Then I'll come to you.' James came towards her and she couldn't move. She couldn't breathe either.

He steadied her chin, as he had done when he wiped away her tears, but now the dark head bowed and his lips brushed her trembling mouth. He touched her nowhere else but as the kiss deepened rising heat wrapped her whole body.

ONCE A
CHEAT

BY

JANE DONNELLY

MILLS & BOON LIMITED
ETON HOUSE   18–24 PARADISE ROAD
RICHMOND   SURREY   TW9 1SR

*First published in Great Britain 1991
by Mills & Boon Limited*

© Jane Donnelly 1991

*Australian copyright 1991
Philippine copyright 1991
This edition 1991*

ISBN 0 263 77270 5

*Set in 10 on 12 pt Linotron Times
01-9110-53656
Typeset in Great Britain by Centracet, Cambridge
Made and printed in Great Britain*

CHAPTER ONE

STANDING in the wings of the Kenston Little Theatre on the Green waiting for her cue, Rosalyn Becket, hair drawn demurely back and wearing a grey long-sleeved ankle-length dress, was hyping herself out of her worries.

It had been one of those days. Rosalyn's naturally high spirits had been damped down into mild depression but, as always, when she stepped on to the stage the play became her world and she became another woman.

This month she was Becky Sharp; the play was based on Thackeray's *Vanity Fair*, and as she moved into the scene where the pupils of Miss Pinkerton's Academy were saying goodbye to each other, their schooldays over, she smiled a sly little smile. The others were wondering what lay ahead but Rebecca Sharp had her future planned.

Not a nice girl, Becky, cold-hearted and conniving, but the audience enjoyed her wicked ways, and when the play was over and the cast were making their bows she got some enthusiastic applause.

Rosayln always did. This was a young and talented company, but as an actress Rosalyn Becket had an incandescence that shone like a spotlight so that audiences could hardly keep their eyes off her. Off stage she was an attractive girl, but all her really exciting emotional experiences seemed to happen on stage.

Tonight, as Becky, she had blazed and burned, and now her head swam and she clutched the hand of the actor who was leading her forward for a final bow. 'Went all right, didn't it?' he said through the flashing smile he was directing into the auditorium. 'Tell Lou I'll see her as soon as I've got this lot off.'

'This lot' was the uniform of an officer in the Guards at the time of Waterloo, and Louise and Rosalyn shared a dressing-room here and a flat in town. In the early hours of this morning Louise had been moaning to Rosalyn that she and Roddy were definitely through, but Rosalyn murmured, 'I'll tell her,' and looked for Jeremy in the audience.

He would be somewhere in the theatre, because they were having supper together. Rosalyn could never eat before a performance and the final curtain always left her too drained for any appetite at all, but by the time they had walked to the Tollgate she was usually starting to feel peckish.

The audience were still clapping as she scanned the seats, looking for Jeremy's familiar face. There were beaming smiles and clapping hands everywhere except for one man, who sat in the centre of the third row and seemed detached from the enthusiasm around him. Or perhaps he had been applauding and had just stopped. But now he was looking steadily at Rosalyn and his dark sardonic face was spoiling her moment of triumph.

They operated on a tight budget here, so this had to be a cheapjack production. The ball on the eve of Waterloo had been music off stage and couples seen through an archway, coming out on to a balcony to say their lines. Those kind of tricks gave the illusion of a large cast and lavish settings. But it *had* gone well, even if the make-believe had not worked for him.

As the curtain came down Rosalyn frowned, wondering why all those satisfied customers hadn't outweighed one man sitting there like judge and jury. What did he expect for the price of their tickets? You could buy a season here for less than a single London production and she wished she could point that out to him. She had only met his eyes for a moment but he had shaken her so badly that she couldn't remember now whether or not she had spotted Jeremy's fair thatch of hair and the gleam of his spectacles.

But Jeremy would be along, no doubt about that. The persistence of Jeremy Hiatt was becoming one of Rosalyn's real-life worries, because although she liked him very much his idea of what their relationship meant differed from hers.

He thought he was in love with her. He might be. She might be in love with him; they got on famously, but he had started talking about their future together and that scared her. Her future was following a wandering star. She was not ready for commitment to any man and her problem was how to make Jeremy understand this without hurting him.

So far she had smiled and kept it light, but she was going to have to say, Don't get too serious about me because I won't be around that long, and tonight could be the night. She had said it before, but this time he must understand that she meant it, and then she hoped they could go on in a pleasant way, enjoying each other's company.

Jeremy was useful to her. A few months ago he had been waiting at the stage door with a huge bunch of red roses when she had come out with Louise and some of the others, and they had all been struck dumb. This was not the kind of thing that happened to the players of the Little Theatre. They had their fans, but roses on this scale in January must have cost a fortune, and the tall fair-haired young man in the camel overcoat, with the snowflakes settling on him, had looked like a romantic figure from an old film.

Rosalyn was staggered. She could only gasp, 'For me? How lovely,' looking at him over what seemed to be a rose garden, and Louise giggled and said,

'There's got to be a champagne supper.'

'I was hoping you'd have supper with me,' said the young man who was Jeremy.

He had a nice smile, and Rosalyn said, 'I think I'd better get these in out of the cold. We live just round the corner; if you like you can come home and have supper with us.'

There was no champagne that night. Jeremy Hiatt ate fish and chips and drank a can of lager with Rosalyn, Louise, and Roderick Ames, who was staying overnight because that week Roddy and Louise were a passionate twosome.

For Rosalyn there was an instant rapport, and from that evening she and Jeremy were as nearly inseparable as his work and hers allowed. She met no one she liked better, and it was useful to have him as her steady because it meant she was not bothered by other hopefuls.

She had no time and no inclination for the rows and reconciliations that were always going on between Louise and Roderick. This morning Louise had been for cutting her throat, or his, and it had shown in the performance tonight when she had played Amelia, who should have been a sweetie, in a very sulky mood.

As soon as Rosalyn reached the little dressing-room, where the six girls in the cast applied and removed their make-up and squirmed in and out of costumes, she told Louise, 'Roddy says he'll see you afterwards.'

'Ha!' said Louise. But she hurried changing, delved into the king-size pot of cold cream to tissue the pink and white greasepaint from her face, and was out of the dressing-room almost before Rosalyn had untied her bonnet ribbons and peeled off her long white gloves.

This evening Rolsalyn was in no particular hurry, although all the others seemed to be. Five minutes later Louise stuck her head round the door and said, 'Don't rush home.' The flat was small and a reconciliation was under way.

'I'll give you till midnight,' said Rosalyn.

A few minutes after that she was the only one left in the dressing-room, pulling a taupe-coloured sweater, appliquéd with a red, smoking dragon, over her head.

Her 'Come in' to the knock on the door was muffled. She was struggling with the sweater, which was still over her head because the tiny hook had caught in her hair. She was sure it was Jeremy, but when a man said, 'Allow me,' and she felt fingers in her hair she jerked the sweater down, wincing as she tore the little hook free and staring up at him.

She was a tallish girl but he was a very tall man. She stammered, 'You're not Jeremy.'

'Observant as well as talented,' he drawled, and she felt distinctly under-dressed, bare-legged in bra and briefs and sweater. She was an actress. She could have faced an audience wearing less than this without embarrassment. But he was the man from the third row and again she got the shock to the system that had hit her while she was taking her bow.

She hurriedly pulled on her trousers, zipping them up, and said, 'I was expecting someone.'

'Jeremy Hiatt. I'm afraid I'm the understudy.' He had a deep voice that would carry well. His dark hair was straight and thick and his face had an almost Slavonic cast, with high cheekbones, heavy dark brows and a wide mouth. Strong and sensual enough to take your breath away, no way would he be Jeremy's understudy.

'Jeremy had to go to Edinburgh on business,' he was explaining. 'It was sudden and unavoidable, and I'm here to apologise. I'm James Halloran.'

His smile was not like Jeremy's wide boyish grin. This man smiled with just a lift of one corner of the long mouth and a slight deepening of the wrinkles by his eyes. She knew something about him, because he was Jeremy's boss, head of the law firm for which Jeremy worked and a family friend.

She had listened to Jeremy's tales of Halloran's wiping the floor with the opposition, and, seeing him now, she could believe that he was one hell of a lawyer. Jeremy hero-worshipped him, and it was kind of him to come along and explain why Jeremy couldn't come. She was glad he thought that much of Jeremy. But he was making her nervous and the only jitters she usually got were stage fright.

'How do you do, Mr Halloran?' she said brightly. 'I'm——' Then she grimaced. 'But you know who I am.'

He said gravely, 'You're Becky Sharp.'

'Rosalyn Becket.'

'Near enough.' This time his smile showed excellent teeth and she smiled herself when he said, 'But I'm still seeing you as Becky. Your performance was brilliant.'

So he *had* liked the play—she found herself blushing with pleasure. 'Why, thank you,' she said, 'and thank you for coming to tell me that Jeremy won't be along.'

'He was taking you out to dinner.'

He was not asking a question, but she said, 'Yes.'

'May I stand in?'

Louise didn't want her back yet. She had no excuse for saying no, so she said, 'Thank you again,' and sat down on her usual stool in front of the mirror that ran the full length of the wall, to put a gloss on her lips and cheeks and brush quick mascara on her lashes.

Usually after an evening performance she didn't bother with make-up; she had a good clear skin. But she was pale tonight, and she wanted to look as good as possible if she had to face this stranger across a table for the next hour or so.

In the mirror she saw him pick up the card beside the floral display. A bouquet had arrived every week since Jeremy had given her the first roses and they always brightened up the dressing-room. Each came with a loving message. This week's card read, 'For my rose without a thorn, J,' and Halloran met her stare in the mirror with one dark eyebrow raised quizzically.

She thought, You'd never write a card like that. You know that everyone has thorns. She said, unnecessarily, 'From Jeremy.'

'For you. Of course.' He was amused. So were the

others. Every week all the girls read the latest message and smiled. But they thought it was romantic and James Halloran thought it was ridiculous.

She shook her hair back into a tawny waving mass and stood up, slim-hipped and long-legged, a girl of today. 'Well, that's the end of Becky Sharp, until tomorrow night,' she said, but he shook his head.

'It wasn't the dress or the make-up. It's the look, the smile, what goes on behind the eyes.'

She did always identify with her roles, and there was a bit of Becky in a lot of women. She laughed as she led the way out of the empty room into the corridor, telling him, 'You're safe enough asking Becky Sharp to dinner. Next month I'm a hostess who serves cyanide at a birthday party. Compared to her, Becky is just a misunderstood lady.'

'You think so?' His voice could be hypnotic. He could play Shakespeare, she thought. Now his words were underlaid with laughter as he made out the case against Becky. 'She cheated on her best friend, her husband and the man who was besotted with her. Made fools of them all at the beginning, but by the end the game was up and she was very well understood.'

She turned to look at him, her eyes wide and her voice mournful. 'You wouldn't have taken on her defence?'

'Only with the greatest reluctance.'

'I wonder if Jeremy would.'

'Oh, yes.' He seemed to have no doubt of that. 'Becky would have Jeremy in the palm of her hand, but I fear he'd lose the case.'

He would if you were prosecuting, she thought, as Paddy the doorman opened the stage door to let them out into the car park. For months now Jeremy had been her constant companion. Any other man, she felt, and Paddy would be asking, Who's your new friend, then? but with Halloran he settled for, "Night, Rosalyn; goodnight, sir.'

There were very few cars left out here. She knew them all but she bet she could have picked his in a full car park. It was like the man; dark and powerful and very expensive, and as he opened the door and she slid into the passenger-seat she began to wonder whether she should have accepted his invitation.

She could find herself sitting through the meal with nothing to say. She could usually chatter on, but right now she was not looking her best nor feeling her brightest, and what could they talk about?

Men usually wanted to talk about themselves, but she knew that he would not. She was very conscious of the muscular body beside her, controlled and co-ordinated as he drove the car, but when she stole a sideways glance at his profile she couldn't tell if the long close-lipped mouth was bitter or humorous. And she had a crazy feeling that under his clothing his skin would show battle scars.

They stopped at traffic-lights and he looked at her and asked, 'Anything the matter?'

'Nothing,' she said quickly. 'We usually eat at the Tollgate.'

That was a nearby pub, cheerful and cheap. 'Not enough leg-room for me,' he said, and it *was* cramped. 'Do you mind if we go somewhere else?'

He was driving in the opposite direction before she could say, 'Of course not,' and she let her head go back on the cushioned headrest. 'This is a lovely car,' she said. 'Even better than Jeremy's.'

She had no idea why she'd added that. She was simply making small talk, and so was he when he said, 'I'm glad you like it,' because it could hardly matter less to him whether she did or not.

The restaurant was a few miles out of town, a converted Edwardian house where arched alcoves in the panelled dining-room offered discreet seating. 'Your usual table, sir?' said the waiter, and Rosalyn thought that this would be just the place for professional discussions or quiet twosomes. Nothing flashy, but an atmosphere of good living with no expense spared. Very James Halloran, she decided.

And the menu was mouthwatering. She began to feel ravenous as she read it. She watched what Jeremy spent on her, often paying for herself and keeping out of *haute cuisine* establishments. She didn't want to be too much in Jeremy's debt, but this was different.

Tonight was the only time she would be Halloran's guest, he had decided where they would be eating, and now that she was here she was going to enjoy her dinner.

She settled for mussels in garlic butter, followed by halibut steak with prawns and mushrooms, and said, 'Oh, anything,' when he asked if she had a wine preference. Everything on that list would be a connoisseur's choice and her experience was mostly limited to the bargain bin in the supermarket.

The dry white he selected tasted clean and cold, and she sipped it slowly. She had eaten nothing since a sandwich lunch and she wanted to keep her wits about her. This table could almost have been in a tiny private room and she now had a niggling suspicion that the situation might in some way be a set-up.

'Why didn't Jeremy phone me?' she asked.

'There was no time. His secretary tried to get you, and then I said I'd contact you. I'd heard a lot about you.' He said that smiling, but she tensed so that her stomach muscles knotted. 'From Jeremy.'

Then she breathed again, because Jeremy would only say complimentary things.

'I had intended to leave a message,' he went on. 'But after seeing the play I had to come round and tell you how impressive your Becky was.'

Of course she was flattered, and from then on everything was easier. The food tasted as good as it looked and James Halloran was brilliant company. He knew so much about the theatre, always the subject closest to her heart, and they discussed productions and performers. He had some hilarious tales about some of the stars that had her rocking with laughter, and when the sweet trolley came round she took profiteroles laced with cream and thought, I'm having a lovely greedy time.

'Do you have a family?' he asked her.

She licked the cream from her spoon. 'Just my brother. He's in antiques. He's got a workshop and gallery in a converted railway station in the West Country called Heritage Halt. Bit of a daft name, isn't it? But it's a super place; I always like being there. He's all the family I have but——'

She bit her lip, because she had nearly started singing Ben's praises, saying how close they were, what a good brother he was, and that would probably bore someone who didn't know Ben from Adam. 'But we make a good team,' she said instead, forking up a profiterole.

'I'm sure you do.' That was what she *thought* he said, but it was spoken quietly, and suddenly he was looking at her as he had in the theatre, with the same piercing watchfulness. 'You've met Jeremy's parents,' he said.

'Yes.' Three times in six months, at the big house with lawns leading down to the river in the best part of town. They hadn't welcomed her with open arms but she hadn't expected them to. They had been amiable. Jeremy's mother was elegant; his father was a very successful stockbroker.

'What did you think of them?' he asked.

'They're charming.' What did he expect her to say?

He said, 'Indeed,' and waited, and after a few moments she said,

'I've only seen them three times and twice the house was full of other guests. I hardly know them.'

'I've known them for years,' he said. 'And I'm fond of them.'

'Good!' Her instincts were telling her she was not going to like this, 'Well, I'm afraid I haven't given them much thought, and I don't suppose they've given me much.'

'On the contrary. You've been on their minds a great deal.'

'Why?'

'That must be obvious. Their son is infatuated with you.' His smile didn't take away the sting, and she could have said tartly, And infatuation is all it is, but he went on, 'I did have another reason for wanting to talk to you, as well as discussing the play.'

At that she gave a yelp of laughter. 'Don't tell me you're the old family lawyer, here to buy me off?' She still had the tiny cream bun speared on her fork like a child's lollipop, and she dropped it back on her plate and looked across at him with bright mocking eyes. 'I know the lines for that. I was in a play that had that in.' If she didn't keep laughing she would be angry. 'You say "How much will you take to get out of the boy's life?" and then I name my figure.'

'Do you?' His drawl matched the cynical amusement of his grin. 'Well, don't bother, because it isn't that play. And I may be the old family lawyer but I'm representing no one except myself as Jeremy's friend.'

He was deadly serious now, without even the glimmer of a grin. 'I don't know if he's told you this,' he said, 'but his parents are strongly opposed to your relationship.'

Now she didn't pretend to smile either. 'No, he didn't mention that,' she said coldly. 'Perhaps he didn't think it mattered.'

'Unfortunately, from a practical point of view, it does. There is family money, quite a substantial amount, and if Jeremy should marry you he'll see none of it.'

She was shocked to the core. This was parent power with a vengeance, outright blackmail, and she sneered, 'Can they make you sack him as well? Will he be out of a job too?'

She didn't think that could happen for a moment. She couldn't imagine anyone telling him what to do. She was trying to insult him the way he was insulting her, but he didn't rise to it. 'No,' he said calmly. 'And he's good at his work, but he isn't going to make a fortune if he doesn't inherit one. Has he asked you to marry him yet?'

Not in so many words, but only because she had dodged the question. She didn't answer. She laced her fingers under her chin and smiled smugly with closed lips, like a woman who could keep a secret.

'When he does,' said Halloran, as if she had said 'Not yet', 'I presume he'll tell you all this, but I felt you should be aware of the situation.'

'I'm touched. It's very considerate of you.' She wrinkled her nose at the chocolate and cream mixture on her plate. It would taste sour now, and she said, 'This has all been absolutely riveting, and the food wasn't bad either.' She got up and when he stood too she said. 'I can get a taxi; do finish your meal.'

He had declined sweet and cheese but he still had half a cup of coffee. 'I've finished,' he said, and she thought, I bet you have.

'Everything satisfactory, sir?' asked the head waiter, and she laughed at that right out into the car park.

She should have called for a taxi from Reception. There were only private cars out here and Halloran was out of the restaurant right behind her. When he opened the car door she was tempted to hiss, 'No, thanks, I've had as much of your company as I can take,' but the four or five miles back to town were mostly along country roads with unkempt verges and no pavements.

The car ride would soon be over. So she got into the car and sat in stony silence, bolt upright, hands clenched in her lap and her head turned towards her own faint reflection in the dark glass of the window.

Act cool, she was ordering herself, because inside

she was seething. If anyone had asked her she would have been the first to admit that she could not have been Hilary and Charles Hiatt's ideal daughter-in-law. She had never thought about it, because there was no chance of her marrying Jeremy. She didn't *want* to marry him. She had been wondering for ages how to bring him round to accepting that without bruising his ego or damaging his pride.

And a fat lot anyone had cared for her pride. This arrogant swine beside her had sneered when she was taking her bow. He'd lied when he said he'd enjoyed the play and he thought she was brilliant. What he really thought was that it was a cheap little show. And so was she; cheap and so *stupid*!

He'd fed her and flattered her and made her make a fool of herself, then calmly informed her that rather than accept her a couple of raging snobs were prepared to cut their son out of their lives. What did they think she was, a plague-carrier?

He was fond of them, he said, so he had a weird taste in friends, and some very odd ideas altogether. He wasn't apologising for their attitude. He seemed to think it was reasonable that Jeremy should be protected from the likes of her by any dirty trick in the book.

By now she was almost nose to nose with her glaring reflection in the car window, so hot with fury that she could hardly breathe. As the car slowed down, taking a bend in the road on the outskirts of town, she reached for the handle and he spoke for the first time during the drive, demanding, 'What the hell are you doing?'

'I'll walk from here. I could do with some fresh air.'

He drew up and she shot out of the car on to the

close-cropped turf. 'Goodnight,' he said. As the car pulled away, she took a couple of steps and went sprawling over a hunk of Cotswold stone, strategically placed by the householders to keep cars off their grass.

She was not hurt—the grass was soft—but she screamed silently as she bounded back on to her feet because she was sure he had seen her in the driving-mirror and that he was smiling as he drove away.

It was late to be walking the streets, but this was a fairly law-abiding town and she strode purposefully down well-lit roads towards the terraced row where she and Louise shared an attic apartment. Rich food and churning indignation were making her feel quite bilious.

She had her key, but it seemed tactful to knock on the door and wait for Louise to open it. Lou looked dishevelled and sounded truculent. 'You said midnight.'

'Sorry,' said Rosalyn. 'Something I ate didn't agree with me.'

If Lou had been alone she might have told her what had been going on, but Lou had been snuggled up on the living-room sofa with Roddy, with the lights dimmed, and that was all Lou was interested in right now.

It would keep till tomorrow, and after a night's sleep Rosalyn should be able to tell the tale as the farce it was. All that fuss about keeping Jeremy out of her clutches when he had always been free as air. It was a joke, but tonight it felt like an outrage, and the only one who would have been really angry for her was her brother.

Ben would have said, Who do they think they are?

Nobody's putting *you* down. But the phone was in the living-room with Lou and Roddy, and she had already had a call from Ben today; he had problems enough of his own. Besides, if Ben did come storming up here he would only cause trouble. Ben could be hot-headed, while there was a cold, steely ruthlessness about James Halloran, and the last thing she wanted was those two on a collision course.

She could fight her own battles. Tomorrow she would have all this out with Jeremy in blunt plain language. She only wished she had done that before Halloran came on the scene, because he was the first man for a long time to disturb her rest.

She couldn't get to sleep for hours, tossing and turning and fuming, and when she did sleep he probably stalked through her dreams because next morning, almost before she opened her eyes, she was filled with a shuddering foreboding that somewhere he was waiting for her.

CHAPTER TWO

In the end Rosalyn told Louise nothing about last night. There was no sign of Roddy when Rosalyn came out of her bedroom, barefoot in a towelling robe, making for the tiny kitchenette and a cup of coffee. But Louise was dressed, just finishing a slice of toast and on her way out.

She greeted Rosalyn with a grin. 'We're clearing off for the day. See you tonight. Isn't it a lovely morning?'

There were splatters of rain on the window-pane but Lou went off singing a happy tune, and Rosalyn poured herself coffee with a wry smile. This was very much a theatrical affair, always being played as high drama. After a few weeks of sweetness and light there was always another almighty row during which Louise ranted and raved around the flat, and, although she liked Lou, Rosalyn would have been living alone if she could have found an affordable room.

Well, there should be a peaceful day ahead of her. Today was Saturday. No rehearsals, except getting together just what she would say to Jeremy when she saw him. If he didn't phone, or turn up at the theatre tonight, she could always ring his home tomorrow or his office on Monday.

But she saw no reason why she should rush to reassure his parents and James Halloran that the dear boy was in no danger. Let them sweat. They deserved it. Halloran wouldn't sweat; he had ice in his veins.

But she would wait for Jeremy to turn up and he could have the job of telling them what fools they had all been.

Some of it was Jeremy's own fault. He must have let his parents believe that he and Rosalyn were planning marriage, and he had no right, laying her open to last night's slap in the face by that bloody man.

She was going to find it hard to forgive Jeremy for that. There was no question of forgiving Halloran. He was beneath contempt—she was not going to think about him. But after this she would tell Jeremy that she could do without this kind of mayhem in her life. In future he should stick to his own, whoever and whatever they were.

The whole thing had been such a shock. Unexpected as the poison with which she was supposed to spike the punch-bowl in next month's play. Her first visit to Jeremy's home had been for his father's fiftieth birthday party, when there must have been well over fifty guests. She had been introduced to his parents and they had seemed quite friendly.

The next time was months later at a garden party and they had greeted her with smiles again and certainly no signs of fierce disapproval.

Last week, the third and last time, she had met Jeremy's parents briefly. She and Jeremy had been on the river most of the day and called in at his home on their way to the Little Theatre and that evening's performance.

It had been a good day. The damp air and the breeze had tangled her hair and washed the make-up from her face. She had felt warm and glowing, and Jeremy had kept a possessive arm around her while he was telling his father that she was a born boatwoman; and had handled his little cruiser like an expert.

'There's no end to her talents,' Jeremy had said proudly, and kissed her cheek. She remembered now that his mother had seemed thoughtful, and that his parents had exchanged glances; they must have been worrying then that Jeremy was not only involved but committed.

Well, he was not, and he should have made that plain before they began to panic and threaten. After she had seen Jeremy again there would be no more misunderstandings.

She couldn't see him in the audience that night. While she was Becky there was no thought in her mind for anything but the play, but at the final curtain she scanned the audience again. No Jeremy, so far as she could see.

No Halloran either, and him, of course, she had not expected. But during their brief encounter he had had such a devastating impact that she could be watching out for him for a long time. He was one she intended to avoid at all costs. Anywhere he turned up she would back out of smartish.

She backed now, with the rest of the cast, as the curtain fell. In the dressing-room she got out of costume and make-up, and caught herself looking in the mirror, remembering last night and the tall dark man standing behind her, reading Jeremy's card, 'For my rose without a thorn,' with that cynical expression.

James Halloran thought that poison ivy or deadly nightshade would have been more suitable, and these could well be her last flowers from Jeremy. They had had happy times, and she was sorry it was ending badly. She was hurt, he was going to be, and everything seemed a rather ugly mess.

'Coming?' said Lou. 'We're going for a curry.' On Saturday nights the company usually had a meal together somewhere local.

'Why not?' Rosalyn slid off her stool.

It had been drizzling with rain most of the day and they came out into the car park to a steady downpour that made them scuttle for cars. Rosalyn was wriggling into the back of Roddy's Mini, behind Louise, when Jeremy's car turned in and drew up with a squeal of brakes.

'Out you get,' said Roddy. 'Your feller's arrived.'

Jeremy jumped out and came over, laughing. 'How's that for timing? I thought I was going to miss you.'

'We're off to the tandoori,' Louise called. 'See you there.'

They all drove away as Rosalyn climbed into Jeremy's car and said, 'Don't follow them.'

'Right.' He took another road and began telling her what good time he'd made from Edinburgh to here, his first stop the theatre. He talked on, while the windscreen wipers swished clear arcs through the driving rain and Rosalyn stared unseeingly ahead.

'Sorry about last night,' he said, 'but I had to get up there and get this statement. James explained, didn't he?'

'Oh, yes, James did plenty of explaining.' They were out of town now, into hilly countryside, hedgerows edging the road and fields beyond. She said, 'You never told me what a state your folks were in about us.'

She heard his intake of breath. Then he said, 'He told you that?'

'It's true, isn't it?' Of course it was. Unbelievable, but you had to believe it.

'Well, yes,' he said regretfully. 'This week I suppose they've realised we're serious and yes, they have gone over the top. My mother in particular. She expected to choose for me.' His laugh was hollow. 'She usually has.'

She had a sudden mind-picture of Hilary Hiatt, impeccably turned out in her highly desirable home, and nearly burst out laughing, because it was obvious that Jeremy's mother was hot on good taste and only selected the best. Rosalyn would never have been on her short-list as a daughter-in-law. All the same, his parents' reaction had been wild. They really had brought out the big guns, and she told him, 'He said they were threatening to cut you off.'

'I guess they could,' Jeremy admitted, and then stressed it. 'I *know* they could.'

She said briskly, 'Well, there's no need, because we're not serious. You're my number one fan and my best friend and I'm your biggest fan, but you've never asked me to marry you.' He started to speak, and she went on quickly and louder, 'And you won't, because you know that was never on the cards.'

'You're joking.'

She took it from there. 'We're always joking, we have a lot of laughs and I hope we'll always be friends. But do put them out of their misery and tell them there's no question of our getting married.'

'Is it the money?' He was hunched over the wheel, his foot down on the accelerator, and a muscle was starting to twitch in his cheek. 'Because you don't want me losing that?'

She wondered if it would be kinder to say, I can't rob you of your inheritance, rather than say, I don't want you. She said, 'Slow down. It's a straight road but it's a lousy night,' but he didn't seem to hear her.

His voice was high and ragged. 'I don't care about the estate. All I care about is you. I love you, I'm crazy for you. I've wanted to marry you ever since I gave you the roses.' He shoved up the spectacles he only wore for distance into his hair, and stared at her with desperate eyes. 'I want to be with you always. I thought you felt——'

'For heaven's sake watch the road!' she shrieked.

They were well over the speed limit and the lights of another car were coming for them. She never knew whether she grabbed him or whether he lost control on the skid-pan surface. But suddenly they were slewing sideways, bumping over the grass verge, plunging through the hedge and rolling over and over down the hillside, being hurled around like the limp contents of a spin-drier.

She didn't lose consciousness. When the car juddered still they were tilted at a crazy angle and Jeremy had slumped to one side. She was hanging in her seat-belt, her head lolling all ways, but she knew what had happened. She freed herself frantically, sobbing, 'Wake up, please move, we've got to move.'

He was lying over his seat-belt socket. She had to push him aside to release him and she shoved with all her might and sobbed again when the spring worked and the belt loosened. The smell of leaking petrol was terrifying. His door was jammed into the earth; hers was overhead. She got that open and somehow she lifted, heaved and dragged him up so that they both tumbled out together.

Two men were running down the hillside towards them. As they neared one shouted, 'Petrol,' and she screamed.

'I know, I know, I'm all right, help him.'

Jeremy was sitting up groggily and the two men grabbed and dragged him. Rosalyn stumbled, getting away fast, but before they reached the top of the hill the car went up like a bomb.

They fell in a huddle, as if they were under shell-fire, and turned to look at the inferno from which two of them had escaped with seconds to spare. Rosalyn closed her eyes, sick to her stomach. Flames out of control always filled her with horror. Now a woman was running down the hillside and one of the men shouted, 'They're all out. There is nobody else in there, is there?'

'No,' Rosalyn croaked.

They were carrying Jeremy. The woman took Rosalyn's arm and other cars had drawn up along the grass verges. Through the window of one a man called, 'I've rung for an ambulance.'

The woman steered Rosalyn into a seat and she slumped with her head down on her arms, so shocked that all the noise and confusion was just a roaring in her ears. Until, quite soon, she heard the sirens that meant the police and the ambulance.

They were so lucky. They had come so close to ending in that blazing pyre that seemed to be lighting up the sky for miles around. In the ambulance Rosalyn drifted in and out of awareness. Mostly it was a nightmare in which every muscle was aching and her head was pounding with pain.

When the mist cleared she asked about Jeremy and reassuring voices told her he was fine. But she saw how still he lay on the stretcher as they were both carried into the hospital, and struggled to sit up and call his name.

The following night and day seemed to last forever. At the end of all the tests Rosalyn was pronounced to be suffering from nothing more than strains and sprains and a massive shake-up. And they could say that again about the shake-up.

Jeremy they were a little less sanguine about. He had a couple of cracked ribs but it was the frontal blow on the head that had them worried. When Rosalyn was allowed in to see him his parents were with him, his mother sitting close to his bedside and watching him breathe as if she still expected the breathing to stop.

He smiled wanly at Rosalyn. 'I've been asking about you. It's good to see you on your feet.'

'You don't look too bad yourself.' Neither of them looked too good but they were both aware of what might have been.

'I can remember the car skidding and the next thing I knew it was on fire and I was being lifted into the ambulance.' Jeremy said. 'How did I get out of the car?'

'I shoved you out.'

'Thanks.'

She pulled a funny face. 'I nearly said, any time.'

That made him smile again. 'Once was enough,' he said, but it was no joke and she was feeling guilty. It had been partly her fault that he was driving so recklessly. She should never have started an emotive discussion with a man who was tired—having driven most of the day—and was still at the wheel of a powerful car when road conditions were appalling. And she was almost sure that she had grabbed his arm.

He asked, 'Are they letting you out?'

'Yes.' Lou and Kevin, the producer-manager, were in Reception now. Kevin had a roomy, confortable car and Rosalyn was under doctor's orders to go home and rest. She said, 'I have to go; they're waiting for me. See you.' She backed out, smiling, and leaned on the wall just outside the door, because she was weak and feeling sick. When Jeremy's mother touched her arm she flinched; bruises were coming out all over.

But Rosalyn's face was unmarked, while Hilary Hiatt looked haggard and twenty years older. Her voice was so choked that she sounded like an old woman. 'You could have got out quicker by yourself. It was very brave of you.'

'We were lucky. The seat-belts hadn't jammed and the door opened.'

'But you saved my son's life.' She had probably caused the accident, and afterwards she had acted instinctively—she didn't feel she deserved the blaze of gratitude that was transfiguring Jeremy's mother, who was clutching Rosalyn's hand as if she was about to kiss it. 'Where are you going now?' Hilary asked.

'To my digs.' To her little bedroom and her little bed. Another girl who knew the part well enough would play Becky while Rosalyn waited for the results of her massive shake-up to subside.

'Come to us,' Hilary urged. 'We're taking Jeremy

home tomorrow. But he'd get better quicker if you were near. I'm sure he would. Oh, please do.'

'I don't think so, thank you,' said Rosalyn. Getting down the long corridor was quite an ordeal with Hilary hanging on to her. When she walked into the Reception area and Lou and Kevin saw her they were both horrified.

Kevin spoke first in a rush of sympathy. 'Oh, you poor old darling. Oh, you do look rotten.'

'You look a lot worse than you did in bed,' Lou gasped. 'Can't they keep you in?'

'No, they can't.' Rosalyn steadied herself by holding the back of a chair. 'There's the usual bed shortage and I'm no emergency.'

She could easily faint, and that might make her an emergency for another hour or two. But it was not hospital treatment she needed, just convalescence, although she was bound to be a burden on Lou and her friends. Beside her Hilary Hiatt announced firmly, 'She's coming home with us; we're getting a nurse in,' and Lou and Kevin both beamed, Lou with open relief.

Rosalyn simply hadn't the strength to argue. If it would help Jeremy's recovery to have her around maybe she owed him that, and compared to the flat the Hiatt house would be like a nursing home run as if it were a five-star hotel.

She would be fighting fit again after just a few days there, but right now she could only say, 'If you're quite sure, thank you,' and sink down into a seat and let somebody else get on with the arrangements.

They gave her pills and she slept well that night. Waking in this guest-room was a tonic in itself. Everything was so serene and peaceful that so long as she lay

still she could almost believe that nothing had happened to her. But as soon as she moved she started to
ache. And when she looked at herself she saw the livid
bruise marks. All sorts of muscles were tender, but
they had seemed pretty certain that no bones were
broken and her face had escaped altogether. Nose and
teeth were intact and everything would mend itself
quite soon.

The girl who brought in a breakfast tray had seen
her at the theatre and it was a little ego boost to be
asked for her autograph.

Her next visitor, while she was sipping her orange
juice, was Jeremy's mother. Jeremy was coming home
that afternoon, he had had a good night, and Hilary
was no longer haggard. She was grave but she looked
beautiful and elegant again and her eyes, fixed on
Rosalyn, were glowing. 'His father and I will never
forget what we owe you,' she said huskily.

Rosalyn tried to explain about the two men running
down the hill. 'They knew the petrol was leaking but
they were coming to get us out.'

'Only they couldn't have done it in time,' said Hilary.
'You could have got yourself out but they couldn't
have saved Jeremy. Now. . .' this morning she was her
brisk and bossy self again. '. . . Nurse will be coming
up to see you and help you wash. The bathroom is
through there.' She indicated a door covered in the
same cream damask as the walls. 'And your friend will
be bringing a case round with things you might need.
And you must rest.'

At this moment that was all Rosalyn felt up to doing.
All day she was cosseted. At home she would have
been feeling wretched, whereas here, although she was

certainly under par, everything was made as luxuriously easy for her as possible.

In the late afternoon Hilary took her in to see Jeremy. He was propped up in bed but looking quite cheerful, especially when she insisted she was being fussed under false pretences because all she had to show was bruises.

'Bruises?' There was a central blue mark on his forehead vanishing into his hairline, but he could see no marks on Rosalyn.

'Underneath all this. . .' she was wearing a long-sleeved dress that Louise had brought her '. . . I'm not a pretty sight.'

'You're always a pretty sight.'

'That silver tongue is going to get you into trouble.' This was the kind of nonsense they usually talked.

Hilary said, 'Five minutes, no longer—that's right, isn't it, Nurse?'

Nurse nodded and smiled.

'Then perhaps if you feel up to it, Rosalyn, you'll join us downstairs for a while?'

'I'd like that,' said Rosalyn. She was in a lovely room but a change of scene would be nice, and she hoped to manage without sleeping pills tonight so some gentle exercise might help.

The nurse went out with Mrs Hiatt and Rosalyn asked, 'How *do* you feel?'

'A bit of a headache. Nothing really, when you think——'

When you thought of the flames. She shivered in the warm room and said, 'You remember skidding. Do you remember what we were talking about before?'

'Oh, yes.'

That was a relief. While he was injured it would have been heartless to break the news that she was not in love with him. She was glad he remembered she had told him that.

'You don't want to marry me,' he said. The muscle twitched again in his cheek and he ran his fingertips across his forehead, stopping at the bruise, and she begged,

'Please don't be upset. It doesn't matter. Don't think about it.'

'I won't.' He let his hand fall and closed his eyes. Then he opened his eyes with the hint of a smile. 'I won't think about it. I haven't asked you and you haven't said no. Just friends, like we were, eh?'

They could neither of them handle a big scene yet. They both needed a healing time of peace and quiet, and she said, 'We'll always be friends.'

'So what will they do at the theatre without you?' Jeremy changed the subject.

'Kim will play Becky.'

'They'll all want their money back.'

She laughed, 'No, they won't, and if they did they wouldn't get it.'

Downstairs, first in the big drawing-room and then in the dining-room, Charles and Hilary Hiatt treated her with so much consideration that it was embarrassing. Charles, an imposing figure with silvering hair and a grey suit cut superbly to hide a paunch, actually carried a footstool across the room and set her feet on it. When the dinner was served Rosalyn fumbled with a bruised hand, and Hilary asked solicitously, 'Can you manage?' as if she was more than prepared to cut up the veal escalopes and feed Rosalyn.

The accident had dramatically changed their opinion of her. She was a heroine tonight. From time to time Jeremy's mother looked at her with a tremulous smile and Charles, answering phone calls, came back into the room and told his wife, That was so-and-so. 'I told them Jeremy's home and he's going to be all right. Thanks to you, my dear,' he'd finish gruffly, and Rosalyn found herself murmuring,

'Not at all,' and, for a change, 'You're welcome.'

They were very kind and they were charming, but when the doorbell rang she looked out into the evening hush of the garden at sunset and asked, 'May I walk a little?'

'Will you be all right? Shall I come with you?' Hilary was out of her chair and hovering, but Rosalyn wanted to be alone. They might bring whoever was ringing the bell into this room and she could not face anyone else tonight. She had a sudden craving for solitude and when Hilary opened a patio door, warning her, 'Go carefully now,' she said,

'Oh, I will.'

She walked slowly. If she hurried new pain might strike, so she went very steadily down the wide flight of steps, across the lawns between the horse-chestnut trees.

The weather must have been better today. She had hardly noticed, but the sunset was glorious, a fiery red orb in a sky that was streaked from orange to vermilion. Near the river's edge she sat down on a white wrought-iron bench.

For a while she could feel herself shaking. She felt frail enough to fall apart and she closed her eyes against the burning skies and began to rehearse next month's role in her head.

She was a quick study. A couple of readings and she could usually have a whole play filed away. This was a thriller by a new writer and she was well into it when James Halloran said, 'Good evening.'

He towered like a dark shadow and behind him the sunset had paled into pinks and greys. 'May I sit down?' he said.

'You can fall down for all I care.' She had no idea where that bit of childish cheek had surfaced from, but she had known who it was when the doorbell had rung. Her instinct had been right, only she should have gone up to her room and locked the door, because James Halloran could follow her out here.

He sat down.

'You're looking very well in the circumstances,' he said. 'One might even say—smug.'

'Might one?' He had come striding silently over the grass and she wondered how long he had watched her, while her expression mirrored the words in her mind. 'I was going over my part in our next play,' she said coldly. 'If I'd known you were here I'd have said it aloud and you could have had a free hearing.'

'Thank you, but I'll wait for the first night.' He wouldn't be along for their first night. He thought they were boringly third rate.

One arm resting along the back of the seat, he leaned back and looked at her. 'Extraordinary,' he said, and she had to ask,

'What is?'

'You are. What you did on Saturday night. Getting Jeremy out of that car.'

'Oh, that.'

'Don't be modest about it. You showed remarkable presence of mind and great courage.' He paused and she thought, Wait for it. 'I passed the car on my way here; they haven't moved it yet.' He looked and sounded sombre. 'Thank God you both got out.' That was a prayer she would be echoing for a long time. 'But I cannot imagine how you could have lifted Jeremy up through that door,' he said.

She could hardly believe it herself. She was fit and tough but she was almost skinny, and Jeremy was big-boned and he had been a dead weight. Terror had temporarily turned her into superwoman. In normal circumstances she could never have done it.

'Surprising what the smell of leaking petrol does for you,' she said, and something in his expression made her throat go dry, as if she were in the dock and he knew everything there was to know about her.

She couldn't look at him, and she steadied herself because she wanted to walk back to the house. She mustn't stagger; she didn't want him supporting her. She sat with her head turned away, waiting for the moment when she felt strong enough to get up and get away.

'This, of course, changes things back there.' He meant in the house, with the Hiatts, and she knew he was smiling. 'You're their blue-eyed girl now.' She turned her head to glare at him and he said. 'Not blue eyes. Steel grey.'

'My eyes *are* blue,' she heard herself snap, but staring into his was making her dizzy. She had never seen such dark eyes and it wasn't just the fading light.

'They're so indebted to you now that you can forget what I told you the other night.'

'I wish I could,' she said through gritted teeth. 'I'd like to forget everything about Friday night. Meeting you was not a pleasant experience but it was horribly memorable.

His grin was slow and cynical. 'You struck a bad weekend. . . Saturday was even worse. But I'm sure you're a girl who turns most experiences to her advantage. They tell me that Jeremy can't remember the crash, so no one is going to dispute your version of how you both got out of the car.'

Did he always believe the worst of everyone, or was it just that he had disliked and distrusted her on sight? She wished she could run but she had to get up slowly and he didn't try to help her. He sat there, still looking at her. 'What exactly are you saying?' she challenged him.

'You want it summed up?' How quickly the skies had turned cold now that the sun had set, but his smile was colder. 'All I am saying,' he said softly, 'is—nice work, Becky.'

CHAPTER THREE

'THE name is not Becky,' snapped Rosalyn, and James Halloran shrugged in mock apology.

'A slip of the tongue.'

Rubbish! she thought. You'd never blurt out anything without thinking. You would always say exactly what you meant people to hear.

Well, she was not sitting here any longer while he played cat and mouse with her—she jumped up and started to walk quickly away, but after half a dozen steps weakness hit her. As she swayed he caught her. The pressure of his fingers on her shoulder hurt so that she gave a stifled cry and pulled back, leaning against a handy tree and gasping for breath.

'What play is this in?' he drawled. 'The old family lawyer turns rapist?'

'I'm not acting, and that was not personal.' Although with anyone else she would just have said ouch, she wouldn't have recoiled as if he had been assaulting her. 'Look.' She lifted the loose sleeve to show her discoloured arm. 'I've got more bruises than you can count and I've got a sort of order of the sash. . .' she indicated a diagonal hold across her breast '. . .where the seat-belt had me. Jeremy has cracked ribs, so I was lucky, but right now I'd flinch if a gnat settled on me.'

'I'm sorry.' This time he sounded as if he meant it. 'Of course you couldn't have come out of that unscathed. Come and sit down again.'

'I'd rather get back.'

'Then we'll take it slowly.' He put her hand on his arm and he felt as steady as the tree, as if she could have leaned against him and drawn strength.

She said, 'I can manage,' but she couldn't take her hand away and she couldn't hold back the tears that filled her eyes,

Everyone had been concerned for her and she was grateful to them, but kindness from him seemed to release something deep inside her so that suddenly tears were rolling down her cheeks.

She tried to rub them away with her fingertips and he lifted her chin, produced a large white handkerchief, and mopped up with a deft and gentle touch. But when she shut her eyes more tears squeezed beneath her lashes. It was awful to break down in front of him when she had never even felt like giving way before, and she couldn't imagine what had started her weeping now.

'Oh, hell,' she hiccuped. 'I can't go back in there with pink eyes.' She blinked, clearing the mist, and he was smiling at her.

'Their pink-eyed girl doesn't quite have the same appeal, does it? But don't worry, they're still blue.'

She smiled too, blinking even harder because his were still the darkest eyes she had ever seen, and she held the smile while she insisted, 'I'm all right now, I really am. All I had was a shake-up but some of me hasn't quite settled down yet.'

She would be feeling jittery for a few more days, and she would have thought that having James Halloran walking close beside her would have had her traumatised nerves screaming.

Instead she found herself strangely at peace. Their footsteps were silent on the grass. The whole world seemed hushed and she walked leaning on him as if he were someone whose support she had relied on through the years. Just his arm beneath her hand seemed to offer more security than she had known in the closest embrace of any other man.

When they were near the house, she asked, 'Do you live near here?'

'Next door.' They went up the steps, and over there through the trees she could see the shape of a three-storey building. 'Top floor. We're neighbours.'

She thought that it might be a comfort to have him as a neighbour, if he were on your side and you could take your troubles to him. She might have said something of the sort, but at the top of the flight of grey stone steps he turned towards her and tilted her face up to his, and her heart stopped.

Only for half a beat, because he was only wiping a final streak of mascara from her cheek, but it took her breath away so that she could only gasp, 'Am I all cleaned up?'

'Not a smear on you.'

'More than can be said for your hanky. How shall you explain that to the lady who does your laundry?'

He laughed, and she still had a hand on his arm as they stepped into the house. Hilary came to meet them, drawing Rosalyn away, leading her towards an armchair, and when she was no longer holding on to James she felt shaky again.

The lamps and wall-lights in here were muted— Hilary knew what suited her; pale pink bulbs were her favourite—but to Rosalyn the light seemed harsh enough to dazzle when she looked around, and Jeremy's mother asked anxiously, 'Are you all right?'

'Just tired. May I go to my room?'

'Of course. You can manage? Do you want Nurse?'

'I'll be fine.' She smiled into Hilary's worried face. 'Goodnight, and thank you.'

'Thank *you*,' Jeremy's mother murmured and kissed her, and Charles Hiatt took her hand and patted it very gently.

'Sleep well, my dear,' he said.

She looked across at the tall broad-shouldered figure lounging by the white marble fireplace and knew that, with both of Jeremy's parents fussing over her, this was a little tableau here. James gave the slightest nod of ironic approval, as if he were watching her perform on stage, and she thought, If I say goodnight to you you'll probably say, Goodnight, Becky.

So she said nothing to him, just included him in a smile and said to Hilary, 'I'll see you tomorrow,' and left the room, closing the door behind her.

She *was* tired. She used the handrail climbing the stairs and at the top she almost sat down in a high-backed carved armchair, but the thought of that beautiful bedroom waiting kept her going, and she was almost at her door when she realised she was not alone in the corridor.

James was coming towards her, walking silently again, this time on the thick carpet. 'Are you following me?'

'Certainly not.' He reached a door halfway down the passage. 'I'm looking in on Jeremy.' That was Jeremy's room. 'If you cared for him,' he said, 'I'd have expected you to be saying goodnight.'

She supposed she should have done but she was exhausted, drained, so that all she wanted to do was fall into her own bed. 'You'd better start showing more concern. . .' he could have been advising a client on prudent conduct '. . .or you're going to lose some of that doting indulgence you were basking in just now.'

He had to be the most insufferable man she had ever met. It took all her control to answer him civilly, almost sweetly, 'Do please give him my love and tell him I don't want to disturb him again tonight.'

'Very thoughtful of you.' She was sure he knew that she had walked past Jeremy's door hardly thinking of him at all. Jeremy was getting better, the nurse was with him, and he was probably sleeping. If he wanted to see Rosalyn they knew where to find her.

But if she had cared deeply she would have opened his door and looked in, just to see him sleeping, and it was maddening that she should have given James Halloran the opportunity to tell her how thoughtless she was.

She went to the bathroom leading from her bedroom, undressed and washed slowly, sitting down every time her head began to swim, which seemed to happen after the slightest effort. She was a wreck, battered in body and mind. The car crash had knocked her right off balance or that lunacy in the garden could never have happened. First the weeping jag, then the crazy idea that so long as she held on to that man she was safe.

She wondered now why he had got her back into the house without letting her fall, when he obviously enjoyed seeing her trip up. Why he had bothered mopping the tears away. Common courtesy perhaps, but he was no gentleman, although she had no doubt he could pass for one in any company.

When Jeremy had talked about him it had always been about work, and she had just listened and agreed that James Halloran sounded professionally formidable. In his private life she knew nothing about him, except that he was close enough to the Hiatts to concern himself with their affairs, and that he was a womaniser.

She would stake her life on that. He had the macho virility of Othello, although jealousy would never destroy him. Never disturb him either, she reckoned. But he knew his way around women; even his casual touch could get under your skin.

She had slipped carefully into one of the nightshirts Lou had brought, and equally cautiously between the sheets. Her muscles were aching and her bruises were tender, but when she lay still her overriding sensation was the memory of cool cotton and lightly brushing fingers against her flushed cheeks.

She raised her head at the tap on the door and the nurse came bustling in. 'Is he all right?' Rosalyn asked.

'Settled down nicely,' said the nurse. 'Now, how about you?'

'I'm fine, thanks.'

'There's a good girl.' Nurse approved of patients who caused no trouble and didn't feel sorry for themselves. 'I've brought your pills.' She went to fill a glass of water in the bathroom and Rosayln called,

'I don't think I'll need any tonight.'

'No? Well, I'll leave them.' She put down the glass and two pills, a large flat one that was a painkiller, and a small round sleeping pill. 'And you see how you go on. Do you want the curtains drawn?'

There were stars in the sky. It was a fine clear night.

'No, thank you,' Rosalyn said, and the door closed behind the rustle of the nurse's starched apron.

Sitting up in bed, Rosalyn looked out of the window. This room was at the side of the house. Between the trees there were lights from windows in the building where James Halloran lived, and as she watched top floor lights came on.

It gave her quite a shock. It was pure chance of timing, of course, but she had been staring at the dark above the second floor when three long windows suddenly lit up. Instinctively she ducked down as if he had caught her spying on him. Then told herself that she really was losing her wits, because this room was in darkness and there was too much distance between the buildings for either to give insight into the other unless you were using binoculars.

The windows were only little lozenges of brightness, but she plumped up her pillows and settled herself sideways, watching the lights. That would be a good-sized room, the main room maybe. It probably meant that he was back home, but the apartment need not have been empty before. Other rooms would have windows on other sides of the house.

What kind of apartment was it? she wondered, and imagined him walking around behind those windows. A big man who made no noise, who would never bluster or shout, but who could be more dangerous than any bully.

He was not on her side, that was for sure. He thought she was an opportunist and so she was, but her ambitions did not include becoming Charles's and

Hilary's darling daughter. Or anybody's darling, come to that.

Did James Halloran have a darling? He had women, of course, and while they were in favour he probably treated them well enough. He could have a wife. How old was he? Mid-thirties? Mrs James Halloran might be over there waiting for him, in the penthouse flat, and what would she be like?

And what was this all about? Why was she filling her head with things that did not concern her, like whether James Halloran had a wife? She needed to rest, and she had to be tired. She turned away from the window, closing her eyes, but after a few minutes she sat up and reached for the glass of water and the sleeping pill. It seemed the only way to tranquillise her mind, and it was all his fault.

She gulped down the pill, put down the glass with a little bang, and muttered, 'That's the last time you make me do anything,' as if, even when she couldn't see or hear him, James Halloran was still pushing her around.

She would have slept less soundly without the drug but she might have woken feeling brighter. Not with a headache exactly, but heaviness weighed down her eyelids so that she answered Sally's knock on the door still half asleep.

Sally, the Hiatts' maid and Rosalyn Becket's fan, put down the breakfast tray on the bedside and declared, 'They've been ringing her.'

'What?' Rosalyn struggled to sit up. 'Who?'

'The *Chronicle*.' That would be the *Kenston Chronicle*, the local paper. 'They want to talk to you but, she doesn't like reporters.' She pulled a face. 'Invasion of privacy, she calls them.'

Free publicity, Kevin and the rest would call it. The local Press would have been notified that one of the Little Theatre's actresses had had a brush with death, and of course Rosalyn would give as many interviews as they wanted. Jeremy's mother might consider it bad form but it could be good business and fill a few more theatre seats.

She drank orange juice—her throat was dry—and she took coffee into the bathroom, half expecting Hilary to be looking in. If she did Rosalyn would explain that this was invading nobody's privacy, and then she would ring the theatre and speak to whoever was around and get them to fix a time.

When she was dressed and lightly made up, and nobody had followed Sally, she went along to Jeremy's room. He was having breakfast, from a tray that fitted over the bed, but the cereal, toast, eggs and marmalade were untouched, and a half-cup of coffee looked cold.

He smiled when Rosalyn walked in and she asked, 'Aren't you hungry?'

She had left most of her breakfast too, but that was because she wanted to get to a telephone. 'Not very,' he said.

'How did you sleep? How do you feel?' There was no sign of Nurse for the moment and Jeremy said,

'Not too bad. How about you?'

'Oh, I'm bouncing back. I hear the Press have been ringing. I would like to give them an interview, just a little plug for the theatre, but your mother doesn't want them here. Do you think you could talk her round or shall I meet them somewhere else?'

'That's all right,' said Jeremy. 'They can come any time.'

'She changed her mind?'

'She talked to James.'

James Halloran could reassure her that this was not the gutter Press looking for a sleazy exposé. But Rosalyn could have done that herself and she said resentfully, 'What's it got to do with him? Why was his permission needed?'

'It wasn't.' Jeremy smiled tolerantly at her. 'It's just that she tends to ask James's advice.'

'You're a lawyer too.'

He went on smiling, fondly this time. 'But I could be prejudiced. And she couldn't get in touch with my father. And James is family.'

'Is he? How?' Rather young for an uncle; maybe a cousin.

'Honorary family, I suppose,' said Jeremy. 'No blood relation, but he's always been around. We owe him a lot. He's something special, is James.'

'Yeah,' Rosalyn muttered. 'He's special, all right.'

'You don't like him?' Jeremy seemed surprised and she retorted,

'Does everybody? Is that the general impression, that he is a sweet and lovable guy?'

Jeremy burst out laughing. 'Now you put it like that, never in a million years.'

'Is he married? Or did he have six wives who got away?'

'No.' He grinned 'But I never remember him without some fantastic woman in tow.'

'That figures,' snapped Rosalyn.

* * *

The Press—a young reporter and a middle-aged photographer—arrived that afternoon and were shown into the drawing-room where Rosalyn and Jeremy sat side by side on a sofa.

Margie Machin, a sharp young lady who handled the theatre's advertising and publicity, had come with them. This was going to make a smashing little story, with a picture of the burned-out car already in the bag. Margie was glad to see Rosalyn looking none the worse, although when she advanced to hug and kiss her Rosalyn put out protesting hands and begged, 'Hold it, I'm fragile. And don't touch Jeremy either. Mine's only skin deep, but he's got rib trouble.'

They all knew each other. Only Hilary was meeting these intruders for the first time, and she offered tea and poured it for them, then sat back, a rather reluctant hostess.

This morning James had advised her, 'Let Rosalyn give them an interview. She will in any case; it's good publicity for her. You have no say in the matter and it's never wise to antagonise the Press.'

Jeremy had insisted on joining them, and now Hilary sipped her tea and listened while the two on the sofa answered the reporter's questions.

First Rosalyn. This was her second year with the Little Theatre, she said. After acting school she had worked almost continually; she had always been lucky. Before coming here it had been repertory up north, radio, small TV parts.

Then it was Jeremy's turn, with the reporter jotting down that he was a lawyer with the firm of Connolly and Halloran. His father was Charles Hiatt, stockbroker and local district councillor, and Hilary Hiatt was his mother.

Hilary smiled graciously, and the photographer suggested, 'How about a picture with Mother as well? It was a miracle escape from that car. You must be feeling mighty thankful. How about sitting between them and putting your arms around them?'

Hilary was not too sure about that, but they made room for her on the sofa and she sat down, pulling her skirt decorously below her knees, and Jeremy said, 'The miracle came with more than a little help from Rosalyn. I was knocked out. She got me out of the car just before it blew up.'

That perked up the interview. Local actress and young local lawyer escaping serious injury in a road accident was good human interest, but actress saving lawyer from blazing car was more exciting.

After that Rosalyn was badgered for details. By now they had merged into the memory of a terrified struggle, and that moment of thrusting Jeremy out and tumbling with him. She didn't want to think about it and she said, 'I was dazed myself. I just pushed and shoved, and the men came running down to help us.'

'The car went up in seconds,' Hilary said in tones of deepest horror. 'We can never thank Rosalyn enough. She is a dear, brave girl and we owe her so much.'

'Nobody owes me anything,' Rosalyn protested. 'If I'd had a knock on the head and Jeremy hadn't he'd have got me out. It was just how things happened.'

But Jeremy was telling them all, 'I'd have got her out because I couldn't have gone on living without her.'

The reporter made a note and the photographer took another shot. Then the reporter said, 'You two have been knocking around together for some time, haven't you? This must have strengthened the bond. Well, they don't come much stronger, do they, than what you've been through together. Any announcement to make?'

He waited hopefully, because that would be a perfect finishing touch. Rosalyn and Jeremy are now hearing wedding bells.

'No,' Rosalyn yelped, and Hilary took over. She wasn't a committee woman for nothing.

'Our invalids have had enough for now,' she announced decisively. 'You can see that Jeremy had concussion. He should still be in bed. Doctor said no longer than fifteen minutes for this interview.' She consulted her tiny watch set in a diamond-studded bracelet and smiled. 'Time seems to be more than up, but thank you so much for coming.'

Jeremy's mother was right, Rosalyn realised as Margie and the journalists trooped out after some effusive goodbyes. Jeremy was pale. It had been emphasised all along that he was to avoid stress, but he had been adamant about coming down while Rosalyn was being interviewed. Life with Nurse, he had said this morning while the nurse was out of the room, was beginning to bore him.

Now he walked between Rosalyn and his mother back to his room, and Hilary mused, 'We'll have to wait till the weekend to see what they're printing, I suppose.'

But they didn't have to wait that long. The *Kenston Chronicle* came out on Saturdays—today was Tuesday—but the local editor had decided that the story was good enough for the group's London office, and next morning a national newspaper gave them a half-page spread.

Sally, thrilled to bits, brought in a copy with Rosalyn's breakfast tray and Rosalyn felt that she should be thrilled herself, because she had never had this kind of publicity before, and neither had the Little Theatre, with their name in the first paragraph.

There was a big picture of Jeremy and Rosalyn, who seemed to be gazing into each other's eyes. 'I owe her my life—I couldn't go on living without her,' Jeremy was quoted.

'She is a dear, brave girl,' said Jeremy's mother, in the drawing-room of the riverside mansion where the couple were now recovering from their ordeal. Jeremy's father was described as a wealthy stock-broker, and the almost priceless painting that hung on the wall behind the sofa had come out clearly in the photograph.

Jeremy had already seen the paper when Rosalyn went into his room, and he greeted her with, 'Good photograph, isn't it?'

'Us or the Matisse?'

'Us, of course. I think it's a good write-up.'

She had to agree, 'It's a bit fulsome, but Margie and Kev will be chortling over it.'

That day the phone rang and rang. There were calls from the Hiatts' social circle, Jeremy's friends and colleagues, Rosalyn's fellow actors and fans. As fast as it was replaced it rang again, until Hilary detailed one of the staff to take down names and numbers and explain that none of the family was available right now.

Rosalyn, who would have liked to speak to her own friends, could understand Jeremy's mother's rising irritation as the wretched phone never seemed to stop until Hilary was shrieking, 'This is beyond endurance. I'm getting one of my migraines.'

Rosalyn herself spent most of the day in Jeremy's room reading to him, because his eyes ached if he watched television or read more than a few pages. She went through the newspapers then picked up a novel, a thriller that was by his bed, and gave that a quiet but vivid reading.

It passed the time. She ate lunch with Jeremy and was called down for dinner with Charles and Hilary, and by then the rush of phone calls seemed to be over, although Hilary was still complaining about them.

'I'm not blaming you, Rosalyn,' she said sweetly, 'but I've always felt that journalists do more harm than good. They can usually be relied on to turn what should be a private matter into a three-ring circus.'

'I don't think there are any three-ring circuses these days, my dear,' said Charles. 'Shall we take our coffee into the drawing-room and watch the news?'

Television news tonight was particularly noisy. It opened with a politician shouting his head off, followed by a riot and finally a war. The doorbell rang through the sound of gunfire and James Halloran walked into the room to the background of a bombardment.

Somehow he seemed to silence the din as if someone had turned off the TV. Charles got up to do that, smiling a welcome, and Rosalyn knew that James Halloran used this house like his own home. He strolled in any time. And she thought how awful that would be; him with the right to walk in on you.

He seated himself, smiled at her and enquired affably, 'How does it feel to be a page three girl?'

She could have spat at him. Her picture had been on

the third page but not in the newspaper that went in
for page three nudes. She flushed hot and angry and
said icily, 'Different market. Didn't you notice?'

He grinned. 'Maybe that will be your next publicity
stunt.'

She took in a deep breath to say, You wouldn't
make a bad male model yourself if they were after the
bruiser look, but Hilary wailed, 'The phone has never
stopped ringing.'

It hadn't rung for over half an hour, but Halloran
said, as though he understood and sympathised, 'That
was inevitable, I'm afraid.'

Rosalyn noticed now that there was a spare coffee-
cup, as if he was expected. Hilary poured and offered
it to him. He thanked her and said, 'I've had the Press
on myself. A gossip columnist wondering if I could tell
him if a wedding was in the offing. I said that "just
good friends" covered it.'

Hilary and Charles murmured agreement and Rosalyn
bit her lip. She wouldn't ask, Was that all you told
them? but after that crack about publicity stunts she
thought he might have said, Extraordinary, wasn't it,
how the girl dragged an unconscious man twice her size
through the top of the car? If indeed she did.

'How's Jeremy?' James asked.

He drank his coffee and listened to Hilary telling
him that the doctors seemed satisfied with Jeremy's
progress although he was still getting the headaches.

Rosalyn was getting a headache herself. She did not
think she could sit here much longer with James
Halloran taking it easy in that armchair. He gave the
impression of complete relaxation, sunk into the chair,

long legs crossed at the ankles and powerful hands nursing that fragile coffee-cup.

But he wasn't making her feel easy. She felt as if he could spring up without warning any time, rising in one swift, fluid movement to tower over her and do something or say something that would leave her white and cowering. He destroyed her peace of mind just by being there, and she thought, I'll ask if I can start ringing back some of the callers who rang me.

She had mentioned that when she came down for dinner and Hilary had said, 'Do leave them till tomorrow,' as if they were all a nuisance—which, to Hilary's thinking, they had been. But some of them were Rosalyn's friends and why should she sit here prickling with hostility when folk who liked her wanted to talk to her?

Then Sally came into the room and said, 'Mr Becket is here to see Miss Becket.'

'*Ben*!' It was sheer luck that Rosalyn didn't smash the cup. She put it aside blindly and ran to meet her brother, and she had her arms around him and he was hugging her before she even remembered her bruises.

'Are you all right?' Nobody cared about her the way he did. He was holding her tight, but she tried not to flinch and she laughed for joy.

'Yes, yes, *yes*.'

'Why didn't you let me know? The first I heard of it was this morning's paper.'

'I didn't want to worry you, and I'm fine.' But he knew she had gone through an ordeal that must have left its mark. 'Well, I'm fine *now*,' she said, and she turned to introduce him, although they had probably guessed, 'This is Ben, my brother,' she said proudly.

'My goodness,' said Hilary, 'I can see he is.'

There was a likeness in the tawny hair and the blue eyes. He was only a few inches taller, with the same slim build. He had a thinner face, he was four years older, and he had a charm that had Hilary dimpling like a girl when Ben gave her an admiring grin and said, 'Hello.'

She said, 'Hello, I'm Hilary Hiatt.'

'Jeremy's sister?'

He knew who she was, but it went down well. She waggled a delighted finger at him and told him he was a wicked flatterer and her husband said genially, 'Charles Hiatt, and no one ever mistakes me for my son's brother.' He and Ben shook hands and, still smiling, Ben looked towards James.

'You're not Jeremy,' he said.

The first words I spoke to him too, thought Rosalyn, and sounding just as stupid as when I said them. Ben had never met Jeremy, and he might have expected to find him here in his home, with his parents and Rosalyn, but he had seen the newspaper photograph and there was no physical resemblance between that man and this.

'James Halloran,' Halloran said, and Rosalyn watched her brother's smile falter.

'Pleasure to meet you,' Ben said heartily and James Halloran said,

'How do you do?'

For a moment she thought that Ben was going to hold out a hand but Halloran made no move and their acknowledgment of each other was over in seconds. 'Will you have coffee or something stronger?' Hilary was asking.

'Coffee would be splendid,' Ben said, and Rosalyn was sure that Jeremy's parents had not realised that it had given her brother no pleasure at all to meet James Halloran.

When she got Ben alone she would say to him, I couldn't agree more. I felt just the same when I first set eyes on him. But she would not mention that he had ordered her out of Jeremy's life that night. There was something of the scrapper in Ben. When he lost his temper he had been known to throw a punch. In an argument James Halloran could deal with most men without even raising his voice, but if Ben ever took a swing at him she was convinced that Halloran would half kill him.

But of course nothing like that was going to happen. She was so pleased to have her brother here, and the Hiatts seemed impressed that he had come all this way to check for himself that his sister was all right. 'It's good to find her in safe hands,' he said. 'I have to get back first thing in the morning, but I'd come to fetch her if she was up to travelling.'

'Oh, you can't take her away from us yet,' Hilary protested, and Rosalyn's bruised body shrank from the prospect of a long journey in Ben's van. Besides, she would be returning to the theatre as soon as she was a little stronger.

'We're taking care of her and we do need her here,' Hilary said gaily. 'She's part of Jeremy's therapy.'

Against her will Rosalyn's gaze swivelled sideways to catch James's quizzical expression. The same reaction she had seen in the mirror when he'd read that card, 'To my rose without a thorn.' He thought that the idea of her as therapy was absurd, and when he caught her watching him he grinned, laughing at her.

She ignored him and said, 'That is kind of you,' looking at the Hiatts. 'They're being to sweet to me, Ben, and Jeremy is getting better all the time. I'd like you to meet Jeremy now that you're here. Do you think he might?'

'But of course,' said Jeremy's mother.

She took them upstairs herself, and it was probably because Ben looked like Rosalyn that Jeremy greeted him like a long-time friend. Just as that had to be a reason for James Halloran's coolness. One man loved her, one man thought she was rubbish, so her brother got a prejudiced reception from both.

Jeremy was very enthusiastic. 'I've heard about you, of course,' he said, 'and I couldn't be more pleased to meet you. This is terrific. Do sit down—draw up another chair. Have you just arriveed?'

Hilary left them beside the bed, after checking with the nurse. 'How long? Ten minutes?'

'Stop doing these time checks for me,' Jeremy grumbled, but she gave him a mother-knows-best look and a tender tap on the cheek as she went.

'Mothers!' Jeremy muttered, then looked embarrassed because Rosalyn and Ben had been orphaned when Rosalyn was very young. An aunt had reared them, Rosalyn had told him, although she didn't talk much about her early days. The aunt was dead now. Her brother was all the family Rosalyn had. She talked proudly and happily about Ben, and Jeremy was delighted to see him here.

Ben Becket must be fond of his sister and want the best for her, and Jeremy had a lot to offer. He felt that this young man could become an ally, and between them they might persuade Rosalyn to give serious consideration to an easy life as Jeremy's wife.

Ben was left in no doubt how much Jeremy admired Rosalyn. 'She's quite a girl, your sister,' Jeremy began and when Ben agreed,

'The best,' they both went on praising her until Rosalyn begged,

'Do stop it, both of you. I am lovely, I quite agree, but so are you, the pair of you, so it doesn't need going on about. You must have something else to talk about.'

'She tells me you're restoring an old railway station,' said Jeremy. 'I'd like to see that.'

'Sure. Any time.' Ben described how he had bought the derelict buildings, trackbed and platform from a farmer long after the line had been closed down, and told him how it was looking now. 'Rosalyn will bring you,' he said. 'It's too long since she came to stay—too busy working. Well, perhaps this will slow her down.'

He shook his head at his sister. 'When I saw the picture of the car this morning I nearly went spare. What are you doing with yourself, you dozy biddy? Take care of her for me, will you?'

Right now Jeremy was in no state to take care of anyone, and even when he was in full health Rosalyn doubted if he was a stronger character than she was herself, but he said fervently, 'That's exactly what I plan to do.'

'Nice bloke,' said Ben, as they walked back along the corridor towards the top of the stairs. 'Nice place.' He paused to pick up a silver candlestick, one of a pair on a window-shelf, and examine it. 'Georgian, very tasty. Is he the one and only?'

'Only child, you mean? Yes.'

'Then you have done well for yourself.'

Ben always had an eye for the main chance and Rosalyn laughed at him. 'Forget it. I'm very fond of Jeremy and they're being very kind to me, but this is not my scene.'

'Of course it is. That's a Stubbs.' They were passing a painting of a horse ridden by a man in a top hat. 'Lovely stuff,' said Ben. 'And you've made a hit with his folk too; you've got it made here. One thing, though——'

They were on the staircase when the drawing-room door opened and Hilary came into the hall, calling, 'Ah, there you are.' She waited for them at the foot of the stairs. 'How did you think he looked?' she wanted to know.

Ben said that he thought Jeremy seemed in very good spirits.

'Rosalyn can usually make him smile,' said Hilary indulgently. 'She brightens everybody up.'

'She always did,' said Ben. He was serious, and their memories were of times when there had been little to laugh at.

'Me and my comic turns,' Rosalyn reminisced, as if she and Ben were alone together. Hilary and Charles were both smiling and they didn't matter, they didn't intrude.

But James Halloran's piercing eyes jarred her and he said, 'What comic turns?'

'You wouldn't appreciate them,' she said. 'They'd be too childish for you. They were nursery stuff.'

She looked at Ben, whose grin was wry at the idea of the garret passing as a nursery.

While they were with Jeremy glasses and decanters had appeared on a low table, and plate of sandwiches. Ben accepted a whisky and a sandwich and he and Rosalyn sat down again.

Charles said, 'So you were putting on a show in the nursery; did you always want to be an actress?'

'I think so. I was going to be famous and Ben was going to be seriously rich.' She smiled again at her brother. 'We've both still got a long way to go, although he's closer than I am. He's got a super property and a good business that keeps him very busy. Do you really have to go back in the morning? Couldn't you stay another day or two?' She was pleading, but he said reluctantly,

'I wish I could but I can't. I must be back midday. I just shut up shop, made a couple of phone calls, and got into the car.'

'Where are you staying tonight?' Hilary enquired, but before Ben could reply James offered,

'I can put you up.'

'Well. . .' Ben's smile was uncertain.

'Bachelor quarters, but they're adequate,' said James.

'I have booked into an hotel.'

'Cancel.'

Ben still hesitated, protesting that he didn't want to be a nuisance.

'Not at all,' said James. 'So that's settled.'

'That's very kind of you; thank you,' said Ben, but Rosalyn knew that if Hilary had been given the chance to suggest he should stay here he would have accepted at once. Halloran made him nervous and she understood that only too well. And when Ben declined another whisky she was sure he was staying sober in case this lawyer started cross-questioning him when there was nobody else around to butt in. Not that Ben had anything to hide.

When she was in bed, and the lights were on in several rooms over there, she remembered that he had not phoned the hotel to cancel the booking. He must have forgotten that excuse, and it had been just an excuse.

She wondered what they were talking about and hoped that her brother would be sharp enough to tell James Halloran nothing about her. Nothing at all. She thought that he would be. Ben was canny, and she was sure that his instincts had warned him of what had been made brutally clear to her; James Halloran could be an enemy.

CHAPTER FOUR

ROSALYN woke well before the time Sally usually arrived with her breakfast tray. Her night had been disturbed. She had been restless even after the lights went out over there so James Halloran could no longer have been grilling Ben. Not getting secrets out of him exactly, but maybe learning things that Rosalyn preferred to forget.

Ben was leaving early. He might be having coffee now, breakfast, and she pushed back the sheets and threw on some clothing. She was going over to find out just what Ben had been telling Halloran. When she passed Mrs Beddows, the housekeeper, in the hall, she said, 'I'm just going for a walk in the garden,' then she almost ran out into the road and up the wide semi-circular drive to the luxury apartments next door.

Ben's van was still parked in the forecourt. Of course he would have called in to say goodbye to her before he headed for home, and she heard her name and looked up to see her brother waving from the top balcony. He gestured that he was coming down and she shook her head vigorously, pointing up.

A man, who looked like a successful businessman down to the rolled umbrella and the leather briefcase, was coming out, and Rosalyn said good morning and walked into the foyer. There was a lift, but Ben was on the stairs and she ran up to meet him.

Now that she was here it was a chance to see James

Halloran's apartment. Not that she was all that interested, but she had vaguely imagined what it would be like and it would be amusing to find out how right or wrong she was.

'I was just leaving,' Ben said and she had to admit, 'I'd like to see in there.'

He turned to go up again with her, telling her, 'He said it was adequate. I'd call it fantastic. If this is his idea of a bachelor pad money's no problem there.'

She stepped into the room which faced hers and looked about her, eyes darting, missing nothing. Carpets and furniture were old and beautiful. A couple of paintings were modern, and all of it was good. The best, she reckoned. She wondered if the furniture was inherited, who his real family had been. 'Where is he?' she whispered.

'Taking a phone call.' Ben jerked a thumb towards a closed door. 'In there; it's a sort of study. I've said goodbye and thanks.' He was carrying his overnight bag.

'What did you talk about last night?' That was what she had come over for—not because she was curious to see where James Halloran lived. 'Did he ask you anything personal? About us, about me?'

'We didn't do much talking at all. What we did was about antiques—he's very knowledgeable—and this morning nothing really. But. . .' He moved closer to his sister, whispering in her ear, 'Watch what you do and say around him.'

'Oh, I *do*,' she said earnestly. 'He doesn't like me.'

'Jeremy does,' said Ben, 'and his mother does, and they're the ones who matter, but I'd try to get on the right side of Halloran if I were you. Look, I've got to go. I'll be phoning you, and you be taking care.'

'Goodbye, then. You take care. You drive carefully.'

He gave her the bright smile that could be so like her own. 'Look who's talking. Who's just had the smash? Coming?'

'No—er,' she glanced towards the closed door, 'now that I'm here I want a word with him.'

Ben had been going to ask what about. Then he changed his mind, kissed her cheek and said, 'Get him on your side; you can do it.'

There were times when even Ben was hopelessly wrong. He knew that Halloran was less impressed with Rosalyn than the Hiatts were and that he was a man who might be a ruthless adversary. But if Ben thought that Rosalyn could sweet-talk him into liking her he was entirely mistaken.

She couldn't understand it herself but Halloran's attitude seemed stronger than dislike. From that first moment when he had looked straight at her in the theatre it had been like a blow to the heart, and she was waiting here now because she couldn't leave well alone. He did not like her and there was nothing she could do about that. She did not like him but she had to stand up to him, and while she was here she was going to ask him what he had told the Press about her yesterday. Then she would be prepared if there was a follow-up.

He came out of the study almost at once, and showed no surprise at finding her here. He might have seen her arrive from a window and he might have watched Ben leaving alone, but when he said, 'Well?' she felt that she had lost a little advantage because she had expected him to be surprised.

She started to chatter, sweetly sarcastic. 'Thank you so much for giving my brother a bed for the night. He was very impressed by your bachelor pad.'

'And you came over here to say thank you as well? What a well-brought-up child you must have been.'

'Oh, I was.' She could have laughed at that. She said, 'We both were,' for good measure, and thought she must remember to repeat this for Ben when he phoned. There's another thing I wanted to see you about,' she said. 'When you were talking to the Press yesterday, what else did you tell them, besides Jeremy and me being just good friends? I mean, did you say you didn't believe I got him out of the car all by myself? That it could all be a publicity stunt?'

'Hardly.' He was dressed for the office, or the courts; dark suit, grey shirt, dark tie. He went across to a table that had papers on it, and instinctively she stepped out of his way as he passed. 'You might not be able to prove what happened, but neither could I, so calling you a liar would be counter-productive.'

'It sure would for you,' she snapped, glaring at his broad back. 'Not for me, though. I'd get the damages when I sued you.'

'That's right, Becky,' he said cheerfully. 'But no damages for telling my old friend the newshound that you and Jeremy Hiatt are good friends. That is what you told Jeremy just before the accident, isn't it? When you were turning him down.' He shuffled papers and came up with one that seemed to interest him more than she did, although he went on talking to her. 'But since the accident his parents have changed their minds, so are you changing yours?'

She waited until he looked at her and then said, 'You wouldn't believe me whatever I said, so wait and see, because you can't be sure of anything.'

It was as if she were taunting a tiger, and the fact that the tiger was smiling didn't make the way she was carrying on any less foolhardy. 'I'll tell you something you can be sure of,' he said quite gently. 'If you should decide to marry Jeremy I will personally see to it that the legal situation is tied up so that you never make a financial killing.'

She was speechless for a moment. This was so unfair that she could only croak, 'What have you got against me?' although she was trying to shriek at him. 'You're like one of the family, Jeremy says, so you must think you're protecting their interests, but what's *wrong* with me?'

'You're wrong for each other.'

'How would you know?' She gulped in breath and this time she did shriek. 'You know *nothing* about me!'

'Come here,' he said. She stood, still and frozen. 'Then I'll come to you.' He came towards her and she couldn't move. She couldn't breathe either. Her eyes were wide but all she could see was the man, and when he reached her, looking down into her upturned face, it was as if she were waiting for lightning to strike.

He steadied her chin, as he had done when he'd wiped away the tears, but now the dark head bowed and his lips brushed her trembling mouth. He touched her nowhere else, but as the kiss deepened rising heat wrapped her whole body.

On stage she often acted herself into emotion; off

stage she had kissed and enjoyed it, but this time for the first time she could not have stopped. From the kiss a sensual electricity was spreading, tightening her breasts, clenching in the pit of her stomach, so that she would have gone down, moaning and passionate, if he had moved to possess her.

He stopped the kissing. He raised his head and she could not believe that she had not been crushed against him, that when his mouth was no longer on hers they were apart. 'How long would it be before you cheated on Jeremy?' he said, and the words exploded in her brain.

She could hear them echoing as though her skull were a cavern, and she needed time to close her lips and almost smile. Her talent for pretence had always been her protection, but this was the first time she had acted as if her life depended on it.

She did smile. 'As I was saying before I was interrupted,' she said, 'you know nothing about me.'

He looked at her for a moment, then he said in that deep drawling voice of his, 'On the contrary, dear Becky, I know you well.'

Not as well as you might have done, she thought, and hysterical laughter bubbled up so fiercely that suppressing it was making her stomach ache.

She had to get out of here, and she turned for the door, making what she hoped looked like a nonchalant exit. 'Super furniture you have,' she said chattily. 'Old family stuff, is it?'

'Not my family,' he said.

She nearly stopped to ask about his family, but he had gone back to the table with the papers, and next door they would be wondering where she was. And she had to go, because she had just had the narrowest of escapes from proving that he was right and she was easy. That was not so and never had been. But she was still not herself after that accident. She was weak, vulnerable. He had taken advantage.

She went quickly down the stairs and out of the house, round into the garden of Jeremy's home, and by then her head was swimming and she slowed down.

'How long would it be before you cheated on Jeremy?' he had said, and while he was about it why hadn't he gone all the way? Then he could have told them all, with the facts to prove it, that she was a lousy marriage risk. But Jeremy wouldn't have thanked him for that. It was hardly a favour for a friend, seducing the girl he wanted to marry.

She sat down on the lawn, because by now little white clouds were moving erratically in the sky and the smooth grass felt unsteady.

It would not have happened. Not a full-scale seduction. That kiss had been electrifying but it hadn't knocked her out. She would have hollered if he had grabbed her, and she began to giggle weakly.

She sat hunched, knees bent and head bowed, until the faintness passed, and she was getting up when Sally came running from the house, gasping, 'Are you all right?'

'Just resting. I've been seeing my brother off.'

'Ever so like you, isn't he?'

'Yes, he is,' and Rosalyn wondered if she could tell Ben, You said get on the right side of Halloran. Well, he kissed me this morning, but he still doesn't like me.

She knew she would tell nobody, but she had to keep telling herself that it was something to smile at, because she dared not remember that it had been the first time in her life that she had felt the shock of real desire.

In her room Rosalyn sat at her dressing-table, fiddling with her hair and thinking. Just now Halloran had showed her what she already knew: that her feelings for Jeremy were not strong enough to stop her fancying other men.

She would never have thought she fancied James Halloran. She would not have believed you could fancy someone you disliked so intensely, but the chemistry had been dynamite. And of course she had been unprepared. Because it was the last thing she expected from him it had been like a shock attack.

Next time, if there was a next time, she wouldn't stand there like the tethered prey for the tiger. She would say *No*.

She acted that to the mirror, saying the words in her mind, How dare you treat me like a tramp? Who the hell do you think you are?

Then she pressed her knuckles to her mouth, remembering the kiss and how every nerve in her body had seemed to take fire from it. She wondered what it would be like to make love with a man who could do what he did with just a kiss. That could stop you fancying anyone else. She doubted if any woman cheated on him, and she looked into her reflected eyes and was horrified because they were wistful, almost yearning.

Oh, my stars, she thought, that is all I need. To start lusting for a man who probably wouldn't throw me a lifeline if I were drowning.

'Come in,' she called at the tap on the door, and

Sally was already coming through, balancing the breakfast tray. 'There's a phone call for you,' said Sally. 'Margie, she said, from the theatre. Do you want to take it?'

'Oh, yes.' There were probably phones up here but Rosalyn ran down into the hall, where the phone lay off its cradle on top of the notepad containing yesterday's messages. 'Margie?'

'Did you see it?' Margie sounded ecstatic. 'Of course you did—wasn't it terrific? By the way, are you two getting married?'

'No.'

'I didn't think you were. How are you?'

'Fine.'

'So is there any chance of you going on tonight?'

'Isn't Kim coping?'

'Well, yes, but she's hardly word-perfect. Well, she never expected to be standing in for you; we all thought you were indestructible and this proves you are, doesn't it? You're the girl they're all asking for at the box office; it would be a crime to waste all this lovely publicity.'

Rosalyn said slowly, 'I would like to, but I'm not sure——'

'Think about it,' urged Margie. 'Check on the old blood-pressure or whatever. It is only stiffness and bruises, isn't it?'

'That's right.'

'They'll handle you like glass, I promise. You can write "Shove off" on the back of your fan and flip it up any time anyone gets too close.'

Rosalyn giggled. 'Sounds like a lot of fun. Can I ring

you back? The doctor looks in on Jeremy every after-noon—I'll ask him if he thinks I'd be all right.'

It would be the first time she had asked for attention, because all she needed was the care she was getting. And it was not the doctor's OK she wanted so much as a little while to decide for herself if she had the stamina yet to sustain a demanding role.

She carried her breakfast tray into Jeremy's room—he said that having her eating with him improved his appetite—and as they picked at their food she told him, 'I've just had Margie on the phone. They want me to go on tonight.' She grinned impishly. 'While the public still remembers me from yesterday's paper.'

'You mean on stage? Acting?'

'Of course.'

Jeremy knew that she loved her work, and her performances always seemed so natural that he never suspected the sweat and strain that went into every part she played. 'It's up to you,' he said. 'You know whether you feel up to it. But you would come back here, for a few more days.'

She said, 'Yes, please. And I don't know whether I shall or not.'

'What does Ben think?'

'He's gone. I've just seen him off. James put him up for the night.'

Jeremy hadn't known that till now. 'He could have stayed here. I liked him; he looks like you. Older, though.'

'I've always felt we should be twins. Toast?' She buttered him a slice, added marmalade and cut it into fingers. Then she said casually, 'The furniture in that apartment. . . I asked if they were family antiques and

he said not his family. What was his family?' She took
toast for herself. 'I mean, what's his background?'

'You mean James? He came from Ireland—
Donegal. His father died years ago and he joined a law
firm over here straight from university. Then he
became a partner and old Connolly retired, and now
you could say James *is* the firm.'

He spoke without rancour. 'Oh, we're a good team.
Five branches. There was only one office at the beginning. But James is the man who always wins; they all
want him if they can get him. I'm lucky to be working
for him.'

'Who's he got left in Ireland?' She chewed slowly on
her toast, telling herself that she was only vaguely
interested, but it was keeping Jeremy animated and
chatting.

'Nobody,' he said. 'If you do go back to work I'm
going to have them put a chair in the wings for me.'

That was not an idea that would appeal to the
players—there was no space for chairs in the wings of
the Little Theatre—but luckily the doctor was firm
about it. Rosalyn could please herself, he said. So long
as the part called for no strenuous activity she could
join the actors. But Jeremy was not fit yet and no way
should he consider joining the audience.

That surprised nobody. Jeremy had expected the
doctor's veto, and in any case his mother would never
have let him out. Hilary said, 'If Rosalyn is on the
stage tonight Charles and I will be there, cheering her
on, and then we shall all come back here and I shall
tell you how good she was.'

If I go on, Rosalyn thought. Sudden movement could
still make her head spin, and she was not too confident

that Becky's lines would all come out at the right time in the right order.

She looked well enough. The bruises only showed when she was stripped, and she would have help getting in and out of costumes. But she was listless and queasy, and she lay on the sofa under the mournful eyes of the Matisse harlequin, and decided that she must speak to Margie or Kevin and promise to be back next week. She needed a few more days' convalescence and surely a week off after a horrendous accident was hardly skiving.

'James wants to speak to you,' said Hilary, who had just walked into the room, and Rosalyn's head jerked up.

'What about?' It would be nothing she wanted to hear.

'Charles has a meeting this evening,' Hilary explained, 'so he can't get along to the theatre—I rang James and asked him if he would be my escort, and he wants a word with you.'

Hilary would not be needing anyone with her tonight to watch Rosalyn. Kimberley Jones would be playing Becky—but Hilary said sweetly, 'Do you think you could hurry a little, dear? He is a very busy man,' and Rosalyn went quickly and crossly out of the room to the phone in the hall.

She said, 'If you're so busy why are you wasting time talking to me?'

'What's all this about?' He sounded as irritated as she felt. 'You're not up to three hours on stage in your state.'

'What do you mean, my state? You make me sound seven months pregnant.'

'If you were seven months pregnant,' he said, 'you'd probably be nippy as a cricket, but you know damn well you are going to make a fool of yourself. You could end up bursting into tears if you insist on playing Becky tonight.'

The only time she had wept was in front of him and she was trying to forget that. 'I know damn well,' she raged, 'that I wouldn't take your advice to keep out of gaol.' As she said that she realised how ridiculous she sounded and she was sure he grinned.

'Just what a lawyer likes to hear.'

'Well,' she mumbled, 'you'd be more likely to set me up than get me off.'

'Tempting, but unethical.'

'See you in the stalls,' she said. 'Sorry about that. You should have told Hilary you couldn't go. You've seen the play already, haven't you? And you didn't think much of it then.'

She put down the phone and picked it up again as soon as the connection was broken to ring the theatre. There she left a message that she would be along in plenty of time for the evening performance, and please reserve two tickets for Mrs Hiatt. After that she booked a taxi.

Suddenly she was feeling much better, as though she had downed a glass of champagne. Her eyes were brighter, she was sure, and a pink flush warmed her cheekbones. She went back to Jeremy's mother, smiling, and said, 'I'm going to my room to rest now; I'll have to leave for the theatre no later than six.'

Hilary said how much she was looking forward to the play, and upstairs Rosalyn kicked off her shoes, lay on the bed and felt the excitement draining out of her.

That energy flare had been sheer temper. He had riled her telling her she was going to make a fool of herself because, presumably, she was too conceited to stay out of the limelight. And that she could burst into tears if she screwed up the show.

The crazy thing was she had already decided she was not appearing and now, to show James Halloran that she would not take his advice on anything, she had just promised she would. There was no way out now—she had to go on.

She would lie here and relax for a while. Of course she knew all the lines and all the moves. It might be a subdued performance, but she could do it. She would take a couple of painkillers, and it would be good to be back on stage, fun to see them all again.

She was calm and quietly confident as she got ready. She put on a white slip that covered body bruises; greasepaint would conceal the blue and green marks on her arms and most of her costumes had long sleeves. Jeremy said she looked beautiful when she looked in to say goodbye, and the nurse gave her another pain-killer to take along just in case.

She climbed out of the taxi in the car park where Paddy the doorman had been on the look-out for her. So had Margie, who came running out with the *Chronicle* photographer here to get a shot of 'Burning car heroine returns to the theatre'. Rosalyn posed in the stage doorway and said she was feeling fine and Jeremy was recovering well, and no, she had nothing else to tell them. It was still just good friends.

In the dressing-room they all made a great fuss of her, although Lou had a slight reservation, asking, 'Will you be back in the flat tonight?'

'No,' Rosalyn said. 'I'm staying with the Hiatts a bit longer,' and Lou's smile brightened.

'It must be cushy up there. By the way, Rod's keeping me company in the flat, so you don't need to hurry back on my account.'

'I can see I don't.' Rosalyn smiled, but the small apartment would be more crowded than ever if Roderick was turning into a permanent guest. And waiting for the build-up to the next row wouldn't be much fun either. Not for the first time she wished she could find somewhere else to live, leaving the flat to Lou.

The wardrobe mistress had arranged costumes so that Rosalyn would need as few changes as possible, and they all thought she was a real trooper, and wasn't it lucky that her face was unmarked?

Now she was glad that she had come. She loved the atmosphere and the smell of the greasepaint, and the chatter and bustle of the girls getting ready for curtain up.

'It's a full house,' Margie reported, looking into the dressing-room as 'beginners' were being called, and Rosalyn peered through a tiny parting in the curtain, spotting Hilary and James almost at once.

They had good centre seats and Hilary was pointing to something in her programme. James looked as if he was listening to her but he also looked as if he was watching Rosalyn. He was not—there was no way he could see anything through the heavy folds—but she had a lunatic impulse to yank the curtain open wide enough to thrust her head through and yell Boo!

She was never very rational just before the play started. Her nerves could always play funny tricks, and she moved off stage, breathing deeply, listening to the opening lines from the pupils of Miss Pinkerton's Academy.

On cue she came into the 'room' and got a round of applause from everybody who had read about her in yesterday's paper. She smiled, acknowledging, and saw that Hilary was clapping but James was not. Nor had he last time at the end of the show. He took some pleasing. In ancient Rome he would have been at home in the audience that did thumbs-down for the gladiators.

She smiled her smug little Becky smile and spoke her first and final words to Miss Pinkerton, 'You took me in because I was useful—there is no question of gratitude between us.' A few more steps and a head turned so that she was telling the audience, and James Halloran, 'I have nothing to look for but what my own labour will bring me.'

Then Becky was away, flirting and playing backgammon with the ancient baronet, playing havoc with the men who were falling for her. Until now Rosalyn's Becky had moved in and out of the arms of would-be lovers, reaching to embrace her dupes, male and female. But all the cast had been warned that although Rosalyn had escaped with nothing worse than bruises there were to be no rough and tumbles.

She swanned through her earlier scenes almost untouched, although she still managed to exude a blazing sensuality that made Becky believable. She fluttered her fan, remembering Margie's joke about writing 'Shove off' on it, and looked towards James Halloran and laughed behind the fan. That was an idea, if he ever came too close again.

'You sly little creature, you are too clever,' complained the baronet's sister. And it looked like that when Sir Pitt finally got down on creaky knees and asked Becky to marry him, and she brought down the interval curtain wailing,

'Oh, sir, I am already married.'

Backstage they were delighted with her. Even Kimberley, who had enjoyed being the star instead of two very minor characters, admitted that Rosalyn had an awful lot of talent. And Roderick Ames, who was playing Sir Pitt's son and Becky's secret husband said, rather too enthusiastically for Lou's liking, 'You're always good, sweetie, but tonight you were a devil. It's been a struggle to keep my hands off you.'

She got into a fuller skirt for the eve-of-Waterloo scene, and dusted powder over her shoulders, and she knew what Roddy meant. She had felt devilment, acting at James, trying with all the magic of her art to make him admit the fascination of her Becky.

She had been on a high in every scene, but now there was a break the adrenalin was no longer charging through her and she felt exhausted. Anticlimax came down like the final curtain. She had no strength left, but the strong action in the play was still to come.

Even the painkillers were wearing off, and she had to dance a little, which could find the tender spots. She gulped down the pill that the nurse had given her and stood in the wings while the music played and couples whirled backwards and forwards across stage, so that it looked like a crowded ballroom to the audience viewing them through the archway.

As Roddy's arm encircled Rosalyn's waist, Lou,

dancing by, whispered, venomously, 'Don't hold her too tight.'

'I'm hardly touching her,' he growled back, and he hardly was, but a couple of twirls were enough to unsettle her. When she stepped through the archway on to the 'balcony' a spasm of nausea constricted the muscles of her throat for a moment, leaving a bitter after-taste.

She had to cough before she could speak. Then she got out her first line smoothly enough, and the lines that followed, but the nausea persisted.

She was hardly off stage at all. There were quick costume changes in the wings and she was immediately back into the action, cheating on her husband with the wicked Lord Steyne. Then came the scene where Roddy stormed in on the lovers and the fight between the men. Becky might have tried to hold them apart but Rosalyn stood well back, swaying slightly.

'Come here!' the betrayed husband thundered at Becky when the wicked marquis had stumbled off stage. The last man who had said that to her was responsible for her being here, feeling like death and concentrating all her remaining strength on getting through the rest of the play without falling over or being horribly sick.

Roddy was supposed to tear off the jewels the marquis had given Becky, but they were loosely clasped or pinned and fell in a glittering heap, and he stalked off stage too as Becky screamed, 'I am innocent,' and then went down on her knees to gather them up again.

Once Rosalyn was down she was not at all sure that she could get up, but she did. The audience were applauding and she wondered if this time James was clapping. Surely he enjoyed seeing Becky get her come-uppance, and if he had known how awful Rosalyn was feeling that would have pleased him.

At least she could sit down now. Becky moved to a chair and a table at the side of the stage, writing a note to her husband. 'Oh I have such a headache, such a heartache.' As she said that she wondered crazily if she should add, and I think I am going to be sick. Nobody realised that. The audience couldn't be expected to, but nor did any of the actors.

She sat there, still in sight of the audience, sometimes spotlit, sometimes in a dimmer light, while the other story played out with Louise as the saintly and very boring Amelia.

When Becky's cues came Rosalyn spoke her lines, while the temperature seemed to rise until she could feel perspiration breaking out of her forehead and trickling under her armpits.

It was wonderful to hear the actor playing Amelia's husband speaking the almost final words, referring to Becky. 'Don't have her in the house, she brings mis-chief wherever she goes.'

Then Becky was spotlit again, asking the audience, 'Which of us is happy in this world?'

For Becky, tying her bonnet strings and pulling on her gloves, raring to go, tomorrow was another day; but Rosalyn's only aim was getting off this stage to somewhere very quiet where she could lie down for a long time.

The curtain dipped and rose and the cast joined hands while the audience clapped. Rosalyn had her teeth clenched on her smile. When she bowed her head the boards under her feet seemed to slant upwards.

Hilary was clapping, but the seat next to her was empty, so he hadn't even stayed to see it out.

When the curtain stayed down Roddy, who had taken the final bow with her, said, 'Not bad at all, eh?' looking and sounding pleased with himself.

Then suddenly James was there, and although everyone else was in gaudy costume he seemed to overshadow them all. They all turned towards him as he took Rosalyn from Roddy. One moment she had been fit to drop and the next she was leaning on James, and it was as it had been in the garden, as if she was drawing strength.

'You were right,' she said.

'What?' they were all asking her and each other.

'I don't know how I got through to the end.'

Then it dawned on Louise.

'Don't you feel well? You don't, do you? But you sounded fine, and Becky's supposed to be a bit down after the fight, isn't she?'

Now they were all fussing and Margie was asking, 'Is this for real?'

Everything was shadowy except James. He seemed to be the only one who was real and solid and Rosalyn said, 'I'm afraid so. I'm sorry, I shouldn't have come back yet.'

'The car's outside,' he said and she went with him, just as she was, her bonnet slightly askew, mumbling,

'I ought to get changed.'

'We'll send it back,' he said, and nobody said anything to hold them back, or got in their way as they went down the corridor, out through the stage door into the car park.

The audience was streaming from the theatre but

through another door. The big black car was only a couple of paces from the stage door and she stumbled thankfully into the back seat and lay low. She couldn't be dealing with fans tonight, welcome as they usually were. She was horribly afraid that unless she kept very still she could start heaving her heart out.

She pulled the bonnet ribbons apart and slid the bonnet off, and then crouched in a corner, groaning, 'Please get me out of here—what are we waiting for?'

'Hilary. She shouldn't be long.'

'I hope she comes on her own. I have had enough crowds for tonight.'

'Close your eyes,' he said, 'and try to relax.'

She croaked, 'Good advice. Right now you are the one whose advice is absolutely bang on.'

'And shut up,' he said, and she whispered,

'Right again.'

Hilary arrived a few minutes later, during which time Rosalyn had stayed very still indeed. As she got into the car she started to gush, 'My dear, you were marvellous. Jeremy always said what a good actesss you were but this is the first time I've seen you and I really enjoyed it. Actually I've never been here before at all and it is a darling little theatre. Tell me——'

'Rosalyn is feeling very tired.' James cut off whatever she was going to ask, getting the car on to the road into the slow-moving line of theatre traffic. 'It was a strenuous role and it has exhausted her.'

Hilary had never thought of that, but she knew that Rosalyn was still recuperating from the accident and now she said, 'Of *course*,' and stayed considerably quiet for the next quarter of an hour.

By then they were drawing up in front of the Hiatts'

home, and Hilary turned to ask Rosalyn, 'How are you feeling now?'

'Fine,' said Rosalyn.

'Good.' Hilary was out of the car, walking towards the house, as James opened the back car door for Rosalyn.

'How *are* you feeling?' he said quietly.

'Better. Truly.' Now there was no pressure or strain she could cope, although she took his arm naturally, without thinking about it at all. What she was wondering was, 'How come you were the only one to notice?'

'Maybe I was the only one who thought you shouldn't be up there.' That was true. Nobody else had been watching for signs of distress. 'I remembered the fight between Steyne and Crawley last Friday, when Becky was in there like a manic referee,' he said. 'Tonight, when I saw you swaying into the backcloth, I thought, If she goes down in a faint it will be the genuine article. Then you put your head in your arms on that little side-table; that was a new move too, and I waited to see if you'd come up again.'

'I wasn't sure myself.' She could almost smile at it now.

In the house Hilary was waiting for them and he asked her again, 'Sure you're all right?'

'Yes,' she said.

'Shall we go up and see Jeremy, Rosalyn?' said Hilary. Charles Hiatt had come out into the hall and James went back with him into the drawing-room, while the two women climbed the staircase.

Rosalyn was almost all right but she still felt punch-drunk. James Halloran could be caring but she knew that he could be cruel, and the only thing she was

certain about was that so far as he was concerned she
had reached a stage of complete confusion.

Jeremy grinned when he saw her, still in stage make-
up and costume, carrying the little poke bonnet by the
ribbon strings. 'Here's my star,' he said.

He must be thinking she had hurried back like this
to cheer him up, and the nurse was saying, 'Oh, how
pretty, and what a lovely little hat.'

Hilary said, 'I really did enjoy the play—Rosalyn
was very good, but she is tired now.'

'You don't look tired,' Jeremy said. 'You look
marvellous.'

The greasepaint gave her colour. Underneath it she
was probably a sickly hue, but when he told her, 'Your
brother phoned and I've got a message for you,' she
sat down on the chair by the bed.

'We had quite a talk,' said Jeremy, and that didn't
matter. She hadn't wanted Ben confiding in Halloran,
but she was sure that Jeremy would never use anything
he learned about her to hurt her. She was sure of
nothing with Halloran.

'So what was the message?' she asked.

'He wants you to go down there. I told him you were
back at the theatre, so it could only be over Sunday.'

'I won't be going back till Monday,' she mused. 'It
was rather too much tonight—I can't do Friday and
Saturday, but by Monday I should be fine.'

When in doubt turn to Ben. She had known for a
long time that she could always do that, and it was
almost as if he had known she badly needed to talk
with someone who only had her interests at heart. She
said, 'I'd like that,' because if there was any place she

could get herself together it was in her brother's funny lovely home.

'So how were they all?' Jeremy was enquiring.

'At the theatre? Oh, much as usual. Lou was glad I wasn't going right back to the flat because she's moved Roddy in.'

She heard Hilary's 'Oh?' and turned to explain,

'Roddy played Rawdon. Louise was Amelia. They have a real-life relationship that gets rather rowdy when they start throwing things at each other.'

'My goodness.' Hilary's smile was twitchy. 'How very theatrical.'

From Rosalyn, in full war-paint, Hilary's eyes went to Jeremy's pale, sensitive face, and Rosalyn knew that she was still uneasy about her son's future.

Don't worry, Rosalyn could have told her. I'm never going to throw anything at Jeremy, least of all myself.

She got up and said, 'Goodnight. I'll see you in the morning—sleep well.' Jeremy reached for her hand to pull her down for a goodnight kiss, but she drew back, smiling. 'You don't want to get this stuff all over you.' She ran fingertips down her cheek and displayed greasepaint. 'It's going to take me ages to shift it.'

It did take ages. In her room she got out of the costume, hanging it on a hanger. In the morning she would have to send it all back to the theatre. And then it took her nearly half an hour, first with the light cleansing lotion she used out of the theatre and then with hot water and soap in the bathroom, to remove the very last traces of Becky Sharp.

When she did get into bed she began to plan how she would get down to Heritage Halt. By train most of the way, and at Glastonbury Ben might meet her or she might get a taxi. Although taxis were expensive and that would blow her budget for the month.

But somehow she would get there and she was glad Jeremy had raised no objections. Of course he couldn't have stopped her going, but it would have been inconsiderate to walk out almost without warning when the family had been so kind.

Far from raising objections, Jeremy was being helpful. When she went into his room next morning he greeted her with, 'When you come back from your brother's you will come back here, won't you?'

'Well, yes, for another night or so if that's all right. I really am going to look around for other digs, I'm not happy about sharing with Lou *and* Roddy.'

'Then I've fixed it for you,' said Jeremy.

'Fixed what?'

'How you are going to get down there. James is going to take you.'

'You what?' she said idiotically.

'He has to go down to our West Country office, and he said today would do nicely and he'll give you a lift to your brother's.'

She said, 'Oh!'

Jeremy went on, 'At least that way you're sure of an easy ride.'

That was thoughtful of Jeremy, and she did very much want to get to Heritage Halt to discuss her problems with her brother. But she had not reckoned on travelling down with the problem sitting behind the steering-wheel. And she was also wondering about James Halloran's real reason for being so incredibly obliging.

CHAPTER FIVE

ROSALYN couldn't tell Ben exactly what time to expect her. 'Early evening, I should think,' she said, and Ben said that was great and he was all for her having a few days off before she returned full-time to the Little Theatre. Heritage Halt would be waiting for her and so would he. It would be just like old times. The good times, not the bad.

She packed her case and brought Becky's costume downstairs to be delivered. It was ages since she had had a holiday and this would be a real break, away from everybody up here.

She would rather have made her own way to the West Country, of course. A long car ride with James Halloran wouldn't be very restful. And when Hilary came into Jeremy's room, where Rosalyn was reading snippets from the morning paper to him, and said, 'James is waiting,' Rosalyn almost panicked and refused to go.

He was outside the house, putting her overnight bag into the boot of the car. Hilary kissed her cheek and said, 'You have a lovely time and come back to us,' and Rosalyn thought how nice she was.

James Halloran seemed to get taller. Every time she saw him he seemed more dominant. Right now Hilary was still talking but Rosalyn hardly heard her. As they neared the car and the man it was an effort to speak casually. 'This is very kind of you. What a coincidence, both of us going the same way on the same day.'

'Stranger things have happened,' he said and opened the back door for her. 'You'll be more comfortable in here.'

She climbed in, and he seated himself in front of her, and the car moved off. A few minutes later, when they were cruising smoothly, she said, 'Out of sight, out of mind?' because that was probably why she was not in the passenger-seat.

He sounded amused. 'You think so?'

She seemed to do a lot of talking to the back of his head, although she could still see his eyes in the driving mirror. Now she said, 'I won't be offended if you ignore me. That could be quite a relief because being alone with you usually means some sort of lecture. I ask myself now, are you taking me to Ben's to get me away from Jeremy, or are you planning another go at me about something while I'm stuck in the back seat?'

'I'm not planning anything,' he said. 'I'm giving you a lift because Jeremy asked me to. And you're in the back seat because there you can put your feet up and your head down and there's less risk of you fainting and falling over the steering-wheel.'

Put like that it made sense and she had nothing to worry about.

'And I won't lecture you if you don't bother me,' he added. But it wasn't a snub; he smiled at her in the driving-mirror and she grinned back.

'Done,' she said. 'Wake me if I snore.'

'Do you?'

'I don't know. It's not easy eavesdropping on yourself.'

'Do you always sleep alone?'

She was not saying yes to that. 'Most of the time,' she said airily. 'Do you snore?'

'I've had no complaints.'

She laughed. 'They probably wouldn't dare.'

'And why should you assume my companions haven't the spirit to complain?'

'Now I think about it,' she said, 'I don't. Jeremy says you always have fantastic women in tow so the odds are they're very spirited.'

'But, as we both know, Jeremy sees through rose-coloured spectacles.' That was a dig at her but it was also a joke and she laughed again.

'You don't have fantastic women?'

'It's the "always in tow" he's got wrong.'

'How about now?' It was none of her business and he was certainly not going to start discussing his love-life.

'How about some other topic?' he said. 'We seem to have exhausted snoring. Why this sudden decision to go down to your brother's?'

Because she wanted to tell Ben that she was not sure if James Halloran even liked her, but she was beginning to fancy him rotten, so what did Ben think about that? And because she could be alone there, with no disturbances, to try to work this out for herself.

'Because I like it there,' she said. 'I won't be working again until Monday night so it's a chance to spend a few days with my brother.'

'The good partnership,' he said.

She had told him that that first evening and she said impulsively, 'He's been good to me; I owe him a lot.

He paid my fees for drama school and it made all the difference to my life.'

'You were a sound investment.'

That rankled a little, although it could have been a compliment. 'For me,' she said. 'Not for Ben. I've never even paid him back.'

He said nothing, and then he spoke quietly and slowly. 'Oh, but I'm sure you have,' and she wondered what he meant by that.

In the driving-mirror she could see that he was watching the road. He moved slightly, hands on the wheel, but to her he seemed very still and again she got that uneasy feeling that came when he looked hard at her.

In her career she was always coming across actors who thought they were irresistible, but he was the most disturbingly attractive man she had ever met. She wanted to put a hand on his shoulder now and ask, Are we friends? Would you harm me? But it would be a neurotic thing to ask and he would probably laugh, and what could he have meant except that her little successes were obviously all the return her brother wanted?

'He's six miles from Glastonbury,' he said. 'You'll have to direct me from there.'

It was a pleasant journey. Playing Becky had worn her out and for miles she slept, waking and watching the shifting panorama outside the window for a little while and dozing off again.

Her sleep last night had been broken by troubled dreams, but on the back seat of this car she slept like a baby. Any misgivings she had about James Halloran didn't extend to his driving. After the crash she should have been scared to close her eyes in a car but, with him at the wheel, she felt comfortable and relaxed and in no danger at all.

She was astounded when she sat up and blinked and recognised the tall flat-topped pinnacle of the tor on the skyline. 'We're never coming into Glastonbury.' But they were. 'I must have been sleeping for hours. How awful!'

'What's so awful about it?' He obviously preferred her asleep; it meant she was quiet. 'And, by the way, you don't snore.' She was glad to hear it. 'You don't talk either.'

'I should hope not,' she said fervently. When she thought what she might have mumbled in her sleep she would prefer snoring.

'Do you want to go for a meal?' he was asking her. It was past lunchtime but they were so near that she said without stopping to consider,

'Would you mind if we went on?'

'Not at all.'

'I could get you a meal when we get there.'

'That won't be necessary.'

'Where is your office?'

'Bridgwater.'

'Well, thanks for the lift.'

'My pleasure.' That was a cliché but she hadn't taken him too far out of his way and most of the time she had been out of sight and out of mind. After her long nap her tension had gone, but she was starting to regret those unconscious hours. They could have talked more if she hadn't been so dozy and, too late, she was wishing she had said, All right, let's eat. But by now they were following the signposts to Marston-on-the-Wold, where he would say goodbye to her and drive away.

Only before they said goodbye she and Ben would show him round the old railway station. It was really something—everyone found it fascinating. And then perhaps he would eat with them, or they might all go out for a meal in the little market town. She had been reluctant about travelling with him but now she was sorry the journey was ending.

The market town had a Friday market in the main road and single-line traffic, but the lights were with them and they crawled through. 'Go right on and turn left at Station Road.' Rosalyn directed him, although it was obvious, and beneath the Station Road sign was a small notice with an arrow: 'Heritage Halt, Antiques.' 'That's Ben,' she said proudly, and again unnecessarily.

The road ended in a cul-de-sac and a small parking yard at the back of the station. There were cars parked, and she hoped they were customers because Ben had said that business was very slow when she'd phoned him last Friday. That day she had expected to be having supper with Jeremy after the show and James Halloran had been only a name to her. Since then her whole life seemed to be changing, but Ben's situation was probably much the same.

It was a warm afternoon with hardly any breeze, and as she opened her car door she said, 'I'm glad it's not raining. This is perfect for coming here. You are going to look around, aren't you?'

'I'd like to.'

'We go in through the booking hall. It's a showroom

now—the shop.' There was only one door on this side and a couple of windows but it all looked bright and attractive, the paintwork in chocolate and cream, the red brickwork mellow in the afternoon sunshine.

'It was really tumbledown and overgrown when Ben got it,' she chattered, 'but right from the beginning he worked wonders. He's had it now four, nearly five years. Oh—dammit.'

Behind the glass panel in the door hung the notice CLOSED. 'Of course I'm earlier than I should be. I don't suppose he'll be long, but I did say evening. Would you consider going over the wall?' Doors might be locked that side too but at least he could see how super it was and there was a bench to sit on.

'Lead on,' he said.

The wall was a few inches taller than she was but with a running jump she could scramble over, and she was startled when he lifted her and seated her on top, although that was the simplest way. She sat up there laughing. 'I feel like Humpty Dumpty.'

'Hold your bag and remember what happened to him.' He handed the bag up and she said,

'I've done all the falling I intend to do for a while. If I can't land upright I'm not jumping.'

He hauled himself up and over the other side with the ease of a natural athlete, and she thought, He'd make a good commando. Then he reached up for her and she slipped into his arms and was landed gently on her feet.

She had forgotten the bruises and the stiffness, and although she remembered them now her intake of breath was something else. He took his hands from her waist and asked, 'All right?' and she pulled a laughing face.

'Still tender to the touch, but all right most of the time.'

'I'll try to remember that.' He was smiling too but he sounded as if it might not be easy and suddenly she felt so shy that she was starting to blush. She turned away, pointing down the platform towards the buildings.

'Well, this is it. This is how it looked more than thirty years ago, before my time but I've seen the photographs.'

The little station was in a time warp, from the big Heritage Halt sign to the timetables and posters and the chocolate machine on the wall. She walked a little ahead, passing what had been the waiting-room and the booking office. 'These are the showrooms.' Through the windows you could see the furniture and the bric-a-brac, and the rugs and pictures hanging on the walls.

'The station master's office and the parcel shed are the living quarters; the ladies' room's the bathroom. It's quite spacious.' She tapped on doors but there was no one at home. 'I wish he'd come—I'd like you to see inside. And the weighbridge house. . .' which stood apart '. . .is workrooms.'

They were at the end of the platform now, looking back. 'When you stand here,' she said, 'it's still a railway station, isn't it? They found pieces of the sleepers and track and, put together, there was enough to run the length of the platform. Then the fields took over, but this was how it used to be. Do you like it?' she asked.

'I'm very impressed.'

Everybody was. She said, 'I love it. I helped with the reconstruction. It was like fighting a jungle; there were weeds shoulder high. Well, most of it was done by professionals, of course. Ben got a loan and he'd had a paint-stripping business before, pine-stripping mainly. Only there was a fire and this is where the insurance money went—and it's a super property, isn't it?'

'Yes, indeed,' he said. 'What are you going to do now, wait for your brother?'

The dark brown slatted wooden bench was underneath a poster showing a jovial old salt capering madly under the slogan, 'Skegness is so Bracing'. She sat down on the bench. 'Wait for the train,' she said.

He sat down beside her, asking, as if it was a natural question, 'What time is it due?'

'Quite soon.' He wasn't laughing at her, although she was talking nonsense, and she told him, 'After a few minutes I can hear the whistle and see the smoke. You can't, I suppose?' He shook his head but he still didn't laugh. 'I don't suppose you do much daydreaming,' she said.

'That could be my loss.'

Then she was sharing this dream. She never had before, not even with Ben.

She said, 'I sometimes sit here and wait for the train to come and take me somewhere marvellous. It would be one of those old coal-fired ones puffing up the line. They had names; one was called Topham. The carriages are small, the seats face each other but I always get into an empty carriage. There are meshed rope luggage racks overhead, and photographs in glass frames of places like Blackpool and Eastbourne, and a

TAKE FOUR
BEST SELLER ROMANCES
FREE!

Best Sellers are for the true romantic! These stories are our favourite Romance titles re-published by popular demand.

And to introduce to you this superb series, we'll send you four Best Sellers absolutely FREE when you complete and return this card.

♥

We're so confident that you will enjoy Best Sellers that we'll also reserve a subscription for you to the Mills & Boon Reader Service, which means you could enjoy...

Four new novels sent direct to you every two months (before they're available in the shops).

Free postage and packing we pay all the extras.

Free regular Newsletter packed with special offers, competitions, author news and much, much more.

CLAIM YOUR FREE GIFTS OVERLEAF

NO STAMP NEEDED

MILLS & BOON
FREEPOST
P.O. BOX 236
CROYDON
CR9 9EL

Mills & Boon — FREE BOOKS CERTIFICATE

YES! Please send me my four **FREE** Best Sellers together with my **FREE** gifts. Please also reserve me a special Reader Service Subscription. If I decide to subscribe, I shall receive four superb Best Sellers every other month for just £6 postage and packing free. If I decide not to subscribe I shall write to you within 10 days. Any **FREE** books and gifts will remain mine to keep. I understand that I am under no obligation whatsoever - I may cancel or suspend my subscription at any time simply by writing to you. *I am over 18 years of age.*

IOAIB

NAME _____ Signature _____

ADDRESS _____

_____

_____ POSTCODE _____

POST TODAY
and we'll send you this cuddly Teddy Bear.

PLUS a free mystery gift!
we all love mysteries, so as well as the FREE books and cuddly Teddy, there's an intriguing mystery gift

little handle you can turn to adjust the heating. Oh, and a cord for emergency stops. Improper use five pounds.

'That's the train I get into here, maybe in a "ladies only" compartment. Then as we're chuffing along it changes into something more exciting. Perhaps the Canadian Pacific Line, going through the mountains. Or the Orient Express.'

'Take the Orient Express this time,' he said.

'Have you been on the Orient Express?'

'Yes.' She had daydreamed where he had travelled. That could be why he didn't need to dream.

'So tell me about it,' she said. 'Take me with you.'

The sun was warm on her face and she closed her eyes, letting the imagery of his words fill her mind. 'We've left Boulogne on our way to Venice through Paris and Innsbruck. We have a day-room that turns into a bedroom but now we're in the salon, which is very opulent and very suitable for a special occasion. The seats are deep, velvet covered. There are brocade drapes at the window and somebody is playing a baby grand, music so nostalgic that you have probably never heard it before.'

She murmured without opening her eyes, 'This is all a new experience for me.'

'Pleasant, I hope, rather than horribly memorable.'

That was how she had described the experience of their first meeting. Now when she opened her eyes they were both smiling at that, and she could imagine herself sitting by him in this incredibly luxurious setting, sharing jokes, sharing everything.

'White cloths on the dining-room tables,' he said.

'Damask, of course.'

'Silverware and crystal glasses shining, flowers in a silver vase.'

'What flowers?'

'Freesias.'

When she breathed deeply she could catch their scent, faint and sweet. 'Glass art deco figures,' he said. 'A man and a woman. Naked, but in separate panels.'

'How very frustrating for them. Are we staying in Paris?'

'Just overnight.'

'Where do we stay there?'

'Rosalyn!' Ben shouted, yanking her back into reality. 'I didn't know you were here.' He came hurrying along the platform towards them and for a moment she felt as disappointed as if she had been cheated out of a romantic holiday.

'What was the special occasion?' she asked James.

'A birthday present.'

'Your birthday?'

'No.'

'That's your car, the Ferrari?' Ben enquired as he reached them.

'Yes.'

'James gave me a lift,' Rosalyn explained, and she knew that Ben was not happy. She could read the nervous signs. His smile was too bright, his shoulders were hunched, and his hands were jammed into the pockets of his jeans. He had always used to do that when something was bothering him.

James said, 'You've made a first-class reconstruction here. I congratulate you.'

'Thank you,' said Ben.

Rosalyn said, 'You should see round inside,' and James smiled at her.

'It might spoil the illusion. Topham won't be calling at the station unless that's a booking office in there.'

Ben could be wondering what they were talking about, but she kept James looking her way rather than at her brother in case his keen eye spotted Ben's agitation. 'You'll have to walk through the showrooms to get out unless you'd rather go over the wall again,' she said gaily.

'I'll look straight ahead.'

'Won't you stay for a meal?' She glanced at Ben then. 'We could manage that, couldn't we?'

'Of course, no trouble at all,' said Ben, rather too heartily to her ears.

'Thank you,' said James, 'but I must be on my way.'

She went with him, Ben just behind, through the big room and out into the car park. Outside she said, 'Thanks again for the lift.'

He raised a hand as he drove away, a goodbye wave for them both, and beside her Ben asked sharply, 'What are you doing with him?'

'Why?' Why should Ben care if James had given her a lift? But instead of answering he headed back into the building, leaving the notice at CLOSED and slipping the catch behind them.

'Are none of those customers?' There were about a dozen cars standing out there but Ben shrugged, disclaiming them.

'They're here for the market and using this as a parking area. They walk in and look round but they won't be buying.'

He sounded dejected so he probably had business

worries on his mind. But finding her waiting here with James had not pleased him, although his last words to her yesterday morning had been advising her to get on better terms with the man.

The living quarters led off the showroom and Ben went straight to a rosewood-panelled corner cabinet, took out a whisky bottle and poured himself a stiffish measure. 'Do you want a drink?' he asked her.

'I'll get some coffee.' She left the door of the small kitchen open as she filled the kettle and switched on, waiting for him to speak. Ben was not a heavy drinker; this was early in the day for him. Something was wrong and she was almost sure it had to do with James.

She had expected Ben to smile when she told him she was falling a little for James Halloran. Then maybe warn her not to get too deeply involved, and she knew that herself. But when he seemed to be finishing his drink before he said anything, she asked, 'What about James?'

'He's James now, is he?' Ben sounded hostile, so the trouble was there.

'That's what the Hiatts call him. That's his name.'

'What's he call you?'

A half-smile tugged her lips. 'Becky,' and Ben looked blank until she reminded him, 'I'm playing Becky Sharp in *Vanity Fair*.'

'Is he a fan?'

'I wouldn't say that.'

'Why *did* he bring you down here?'

'The firm's got a branch office in Bridgwater. He was going there for some reason and Jeremy asked him to give me a lift here.' She had come out of the kitchen, walking back to where her brother stood. 'Does it matter?' she asked him, because he certainly looked troubled.

He put down the almost empty glass and dug his hands into his pockets again. 'I wasn't sure about him when I met him. I don't know why but he worries me.' She had felt the same. At times she still did. 'Since I got back I've been talking about him with some friends who've come across him before,' said Ben, 'and they don't have a good word to say for him.'

'What friends?' she demanded indignantly. 'Just what did they say?'

But Ben went on doggedly, 'He's got the reputation of a rattlesnake. He'd double-cross anyone, do you down sooner than look at you.'

She cried, 'I don't believe it!'

'I do,' he said. 'They knew what they were talking about; they convinced me.'

She had always listened to Ben, always accepted what he said because he was her big brother, her almost-twin. Now she shook her head, refusing to listen, and he asked anxiously, 'Nothing's starting between you two, is it?'

She stook her head again, although the straight answer should have been, I hope so.

'Keep it that way,' he urged her. 'Keep out of his way. He's dangerous and he's deadly.'

She had felt like this when she fell out of the crashed car, shaken stupid, and she stammered, 'Jeremy doesn't think so, nor do his folk. They all like him— he's one of the family there.'

Ben's grin was sour. 'Even snakes might be good to their families but I'm telling you what I've been told about him. You're *my* family and haven't I always told you straight?'

'Of course you have.'

'So forewarned's forearmed.' He picked up the glass again. 'You don't have to bring Jeremy into this. You don't have to tell Jeremy anything. Just remember what I've said.'

She wondered why Ben was bothering about Jeremy, and why Jeremy should be wrong and these cronies of Ben's right. When she was calmer they would discus this again, but now she heard the kettle click off and went back into the kitchen to make herself a very strong instant coffee.

The first scalding swallow made her cough and Ben said, 'I'm sorry about this, it's awkward I know, but you had to be put in the picture because you are going to come across him. Let's forget it now. Come and sit down and I'll feed you.'

He brought a selection of food to the kitchen table: a cut pie, some cold ham and salami, cheeses, various salad mixtures in plastic tubs, a French loaf and butter, a jar of chutney and another of pickles.

'We're going for a meal at the Blue Boar this evening,' he said. 'There's always a good crowd there.'

She would have met some of them when she was here before. They would be Ben's friends and, possibly, the folk who thought James Halloran was poison. They must have their reasons, but if they started talking about James tonight she could end up speaking up for him, because if he was not yet her friend he was becoming something pretty close.

They ate picnic fashion, telling each other what their phone calls had not covered, and now Ben went into just how bad business was, and how customers carried on these days. 'Ask more than a fiver and they act as if the bloody vase ought to be Ming. Then more often than not they'll walk away. Last month I hardly covered expenses. I'm giving it till the end of the year and then I shall seriously consider selling up.'

It was the worst possible news, the very last thing she wanted to happen. She broke into a torrent of protests. 'You can't do that. It can't be that bad. You've got a lot of good pieces here, haven't you? Surely there's always a market for them?'

'It's not that good,' Ben said morosely. 'More junk than antiques. I'd swap the lot for half the stuff in Halloran's apartment.'

That seemed to be a sore point with him but Rosalyn didn't want to discuss James Halloran's affluence. She wanted to know, 'If you get out of here what would you do, and where would you go?'

'Might go abroad. I've got contacts.' And then with one of the swift switches from moodiness that was part of his charm he laughed, helped himself to another slice of pork pie and told her, 'Don't look so down—it might never happen. And wherever I went I'd soon be on the phone to you.'

'I know that,' she said.

The thought of their losing touch with each other again was unbearable. As motherless children they had lived with a feckless father. When he walked out on them Rosalyn had been nine years old, Ben thirteen. Aunt Eleanor, who no one could call feckless although she hadn't had a loving bone in her body, had taken the girl and the boy had gone to a children's home.

Meetings had been rare, not encouraged by anyone,

and there had been a time when Rosalyn had no idea where her brother was. These were the blackest years. But when she was seventeen Ben had come back and she always felt that was when her life had really begun.

Her brother had paid her rent as well as her drama fees, and he had gone on paying until she was earning. Now she was meeting her own expenses and hopefully on the long trek to stardom, and all because Ben had backed her. Ever since he'd moved into this place she had thought of it as home. If he had to leave she would miss it, of course, but her main concern was for him and she said ruefully, 'I'm not earning enough to help much yet. In another year or two maybe.'

'You know what you should do? Marry Jeremy and get out of the rat race.' He had to be joking, so things couldn't be that bad and she grinned.

'Don't you think twenty-two is on the early side for retiring? But I can't believe we're going to lose Heritage Halt. You'll get round this, or I'll be offered a part in a blockbuster movie.' She wrinkled her nose. 'Although if there are talent scouts about I hope they weren't watching me last night. I thought I was ready to go back but halfway through I started feeling disgustingly sick.'

She put on a slapstick show, describing the dramatic scenes and herself fighting nausea, wild-eyed and swaying like a seasick victim. It was a long time since she had used her gift for comedy to cheer him up but it still worked. She had him chuckling as she gave a glassy grin, bowing to the audience at the end of the show. 'I've never been so glad in all my life as when that curtain dropped and Jeremy's mother could take me home.'

'She seems a decent enough old stick,' Ben conceded, which would not have pleased Hilary if she had heard him. 'Anyhow, she's looking after you.'

And now was hardly the time for telling him that the only one who had been looking after his sister last night was the man he had just described as a rattlesnake.

Ben was right about the folk who parked in his yard and wandered around Heritage Halt. There weren't many buyers among them, and the sales that were made were small. But for all that what was left of the afternoon seemed fairly full. The phone rang often for Ben, and once for Rosalyn—it was Jeremy. She supposed she should have called him and told him she had arrived safely.

She said that everything was fine here, just as she'd expected. 'After the accident I thought I might be jittery in a fast car but I slept most of the way.'

'I knew you'd be safe with James,' said Jeremy.

Ben had answered the phone when it rang and was standing beside her now, and she thought, Ben doesn't have a good word to say for James, but you're telling me I am safe with him, and I don't think either of you is right.

'Is Ben still there?' Jeremy asked. 'Could I speak to him?'

'Sure.' She handed over the phone and Ben grinned into it.

'Hello, my old mate,' as if he were talking to his best friend. It was nice that they liked each other. Ben charmed most people, and she wondered what Jeremy was saying now that had him agreeing so emphatically,

'That's right. . .yeah. . .oh, absolutely.' It was a short conversation. 'I will,' Ben said, and held the phone towards her.

She shook her head.

'Cheerio, then,' he said to Jeremy and hung up, smiling.

'What will you?' she asked.

After a few seconds he said cheerfully, 'Keep you out of mischief.'

'Any mischief I feel like getting into,' she quipped, 'will have nothing to do with Jeremy.'

'You can't blame him for caring about you,' said Ben. 'I could take to him as a brother-in-law.'

'Well, you won't be getting the chance. What time are we going out?'

With just over an hour in hand she took a shower, and then changed into a silky amber-coloured skirt and shirt in the little bedroom that had once been the porters' lair. She had always felt that this spare room was her room, although it must have been twelve months since she had been down here. The Little Theatre never closed; it couldn't afford to. All year round the company had something on offer, and since she joined them she had usually played leading roles.

She wouldn't have been here now if it hadn't been for the accident and if Ben hadn't phoned last night. She would rather have had a quiet evening with just the two of them, but he sounded as if he'd arranged the Blue Boar get-together and she hoped the company wouldn't be too boisterous, because she was still fragile.

Ben seemed to be on first-name terms with everyone in the restaurant and the bar, and as soon as they

walked in Rosalyn was besieged by those who remembered her, and the ones who were meeting her for the
first time who declared they would have known her
anywhere. She was so much like her brother, only a lot
prettier, and Ben said he damn well hoped so.

He watched approvingly. It still surprised him that
his skinny little sister had developed into this stunning
young actress, with her tumble of tawny hair and her
leggy grace, joking with the men who were trying to
flirt with her, getting on well with the women. She was
a real asset, was Rosalyn. He was glad she was having
a good time, and it never occurred to him that her high
spirits could be an effort for her, that she really should
have been taking it easy tonight.

Nor that what interested her most in the folk he was
introducing her to was which of them had done the
character assassination on Halloran. In her opinion she
hadn't met a man here who could measure up to James;
they all seemed so shallow. But that didn't mean they
were not harbouring grudges against him. She looked
at them one by one and thought, Maybe it's you, but if
it is I bet you've never said much to his face.

Or Ben might have talked to a woman, and women
could be vicious, especially after a burned-out affair.
But there wasn't a woman here she could imagine with
James. There were some smart girls, but she wouldn't
have thought any of them was his type. Not that she
knew his type. She had never seen him with any of his
women.

A crinkly-haired flashily good-looking young man
leered at her and asked if she had any spare time this
weekend, and Ben said, 'Lay off, Duncan.'

Rosalyn laughed and said, 'Sorry, it's all fully booked,' and was suddenly bored stiff.

She wondered where James was and who he was with, and she looked across at a door wishing he would walk in and rescue her as he had last night. The thought shocked her. It seemed so disloyal when she was with Ben to be longing to escape, and with James of all people, the man Ben was becoming paranoid about.

She let out a silent sigh of relief when Ben parked the van back home, glad that she could go to bed now and glad to have escaped another accident. It had not been far but Ben could be over the limit, and she had asked anxiously, 'Are you all right?' as he started the engine.

'Sober as a judge,' he'd assured her and he had driven carefully. There wasn't much on the roads and he seemed to have enjoyed his evening.

'You certainly made a hit.' He sounded pleased about that, switching on lights in the living-room.

They were all right, she thought, but she wouldn't care if she never met any of them again. Still, they were Ben's friends, so she said, 'It wasn't hard; they were very friendly,' and then she was yawning. 'I'm so tired. Can I have the bathroom first?'

Her make-up remover was on the bathroom shelf, her toothbrush was in the glass, and she looked bleary-eyed into the mirror, fumbling with the top shirt button when she heard the phone ring. At once her eyes were wide. James? she wondered, and swung round to open the door.

'She's asleep,' she heard Ben say. 'I don't want to wake her.' He saw her crossing the room and he said,

'I shall be running her back myself. Goodnight.' Then he hung up.

'Was that James?'

'Yes.'

'Why didn't you let me talk to him?'

'What did you want to say?'

'That could depend on what *he* was going to say,' she said hotly. 'And I do usually prefer to answer my own phone calls. Did he leave a number?'

'No.'

'You didn't give him the chance, did you?' She could find the Bridgwater number tomorrow, but tomorrow would be Saturday, when offices were usually closed. She was furious and she showed it. Ben was treating her like a juvenile delinquent, stopping her phone calls, and now he grinned his ever so contrite grin, only it wouldn't work with her because she could do that one herself.

'Coming the big brother, wasn't I?' he said. 'Sorry, but I don't want him getting near you. He could foul things up for you with Jeremy.'

He couldn't have struck a feebler excuse, and she exploded, 'To hell with Jeremy!'

Ben's mood changed abruptly. He always had a short-fuse temper but this was the first time in all their years that he had shouted at her. 'Don't be such a bloody fool!'

She was stunned but she was still angry. She looked daggers at him as he ranted on, 'Jeremy Hiatt's got the lot—you take him while the offer stands. You'll be on easy street for life there.'

'If I get to easy street,' she retorted, 'I'll be there through my own small talents.'

'If you don't get trampled to death on the way. There's plenty of talent in showbusiness but not many names up in lights.'

That was true but she had thought he believed she was special. She gave a small nod and he went eagerly on, 'You could carry on with your acting. I don't know about his family but he seems tickled by the dash you cut on stage. And this is your break into real security. You can't lose there.'

He paused, waiting for her to admit the logic in this. When she said nothing he pointed out, 'Even if it didn't work you couldn't lose. You'd come out very well provided for,' and she thought, on the edge of hysteria, Not the way James would tie up the marriage settlement. I have been warned; no financial killing.

She controlled the urge to shriek with crazy laughter and said scornfully, 'Just listen to yourself. You sound like an insurance salesman. I don't want security.'

He wasn't shouting any more. He almost mumbled, rubbing his mouth with the back of his hand, 'You don't want security because you can't remember being without it.' Of course she could, but she let him go on. 'Aunt Eleanor was a crabby old bitch but you never went hungry and I've been around since. But things could go wrong for either of us and—all right, Jeremy Hiatt would be an insurance policy but he's a nice enough bloke. What more do you want?'

What did she want? Much much more than Jeremy and security. 'I don't love him,' she said, and it was Ben who laughed then, jeering.

'You don't love him? Well, you're an actress, aren't you?'

'Not that good,' she said and turned away.

Ben seemed to have shocked himself sober. He said, 'Oh, *hell*!' as she slammed her bedroom door.

She dragged off her clothes and got into bed just as she was, huddling up against the cold wind that seemed to be blowing. That had been awful. Like being sold to the highest bidder.

'You're an actress,' Ben had said, as if she could live a lie night and day, cheating her man, cheating herself. Lord, *no*. . . No way could she do that. Even the thought of Jeremy's hands on her was chilling her now. She had never wanted Jeremy in that way.

'What more do you want?' Ben had said, and what she wanted and needed to stop her shivering was James's long strong body beside her. James making love to her. The sweet fire of that remembered kiss ran through all her sexual nerves until deep inside her warmth flowered. That was what she wanted, to be so close to him that she was held forever.

She turned over on to her side and clasped the pillow to her face.

CHAPTER SIX

BEN brought Rosalyn an early-morning cup of tea, tapping on her door and, when she called, 'Come in,' standing in the doorway looking sheepish.

'Sorry about last night,' he said, and so he should be! 'I'd had one too many and I didn't put any of it too well.'

She knew he had only been thinking of her. It was a risky life she had chosen, with no guarantee of success, and Jeremy seemed to be offering gilt-edged security. As she took the tea her brother said plaintively, 'I thought I had more influence with you. So did Jeremy. We talked when I phoned you. He asked if you took my advice and I said you did and he said, "If she comes down to you will you tell her she ought to marry me?"'

Jeremy would make some woman a good husband, but they had the wrong one in Rosalyn, and she laughed a little. 'You're a pair of plotters. Well, you can tell him you tried, but just for once I am not being guided by you because I don't want to marry him. And he needs a wife like me like a hole in the head if he really stopped to think.' She stopped, then went on, stressing her words by spacing them. 'Is—that—plain—enough?'

'Yes, all right.' Ben accepted that, shrugging it off. 'But the other advice. About Halloran.' Suddenly he looked grim and intense and not boyish any more.

112

'There I do know best,' he said urgently. 'Don't get involved with him, I'm begging you.'

He was cold sober this morning and in deadly earnest, and in a way she supposed she could understand. Lawyers had enemies, especially among losers. Some friends of Ben's must fear and hate Halloran and Ben was siding with them.

She didn't want to hear what Ben had been told and there would be no point in her pleading James's cause. What would it add up to, anyway? He can be a swine but he has been kind to me, and I didn't know what wanting a man meant until I met him.

She couldn't say that, and Ben's pride had already taken a knock over Jeremy. This seemed to matter even more to him and again she was not heeding his advice, but there was no need to make a production of it. What Ben heard about her private life away from here was usually what she told him in their phone calls. Before the accident it had been nearly a year since they'd met. If she and James stayed friends Ben wouldn't know. James could be her lover and it would probably be a long time before Ben found out. By then he might not be so prejudiced. Secret lover? she thought. Some hope!

She said, 'Don't worry, I don't think I'll be seeing much of him,' and because she was a good actress she sounded so uninterested that Ben believed he had got a promise out of her.

The fine weather brought in a few strollers and sightseers and a few sales. Rosalyn sat on the seat on the platform, with her script for the week after next. Only another week of Becky and then she was the

Lucretia Borgia of Tunbridge Wells, ending up knocking off half the cast with her sparkling cyanide. She
would be sorry to say goodbye to Becky, who would
never have been crude enough to poison the punch,
and she wondered if James would come along to see
her.

She found herself thinking back on roles she had
played that she would have liked him to watch. Local
critics had said she was a radiant Rosalind when the
Little Theatre company made one of their rare sorties
into Shakespeare, and she had had a lovely time as the
sexy ghost in Noël Coward's *Blithe Spirit*. She wished
James could have been in those audiences.

Ben had asked her, 'What more do you want?' and
she had wanted James, passionately and physically, but
there was something else she wanted from him as well.
She wanted his approval, for him to be proud of her.

She was listening for a phone call. The window in
the living-room was open and each time Ben answered
the phone she sat up straighter to hear. If James had
called again she would have been at that window
saying, I'll take it this time, in a manner that left no
doubt that Ben would cut her off at his peril. Of course
she would have been careful what she said; she wasn't
upsetting Ben.

But there was only one caller who wanted to speak
to her. Ben put his head through the window, holding
the receiver, and said, 'Duncan says are you available?'

'No, thank you,' she said, and as Ben bobbed back
she heard him say,

'You heard that?'

A little while later he came out to tell her he was off
to see a man about a sideboard. Did she want to come?

'I'll mind the shop,' she said, and waved her script at him. 'And carry on with this.'

But as soon as Ben drove away she got through to Directory Enquiries for Connolly and Halloran's number, and when she dialled that she was asked to leave a message on the answering machine. A message might reach him eventually but she had been so sure she was going to get in touch right away that the impersonal female voice threw her.

What message could she leave? She listened to the pips and then she hung up, and wondered if she could phone the Hiatts and see if they knew where she might contact James. But if she did Jeremy would be wanting to know why she was chasing him and everything could get complicated.

Everything *was* complicated. As a woman she had never wasted her time mooning over a man who wasn't there, missing him as if there were a black void where he should be. It made her feel restless and useless and she went back into the showrooms where at least she might be able to do something constructive.

A woman held up a pottery cat and said accusingly, 'This is chipped.'

Rosalyn said, 'I'm not surprised; he's pretty old, but he's still pretty.'

Not at that price, the woman decided, but, before Ben came back with a small mahogany sideboard in the back of the van, she had persuaded a few customers to part with their cash. 'I could use you here,' he told her. 'You'd charm it out of them. By the way, we're going round to Alan's and Emma's tonight.'

Emma put on a good meal. There were ten of them round the dinner table and the wine and talk flowed. It was a cheerful evening and when Rosalyn went to bed around midnight she was soon asleep.

Perhaps she had been dreaming, in vague colourless images, before she dreamed herself on to the Orient Express.

There was vivid colour then and brilliant detail, just as it had been described to her. She was walking towards the salon. She could hear the music and smell the flowers and she could see James. He was in evening dress. So were other men, but his profile was clear and hard, and he was smiling, but not at her. At a woman who was a cloud of shining hair with diamonds glittering in it, and James bent his head to her upturned face and Rosalyn felt a pain like a thin knife going under her ribs. Then she was running and sobbing until her storm of grief woke her and it took her a few seconds to realise she had been dreaming.

Not that that was much comfort. Subconsciously she must be bitterly jealous of that woman whose birthday treat had been the Orient Express, staying in Paris, travelling and sleeping in the little day-room that became a bedroom at night.

She should be thankful her dream setting had been the bar-salon and not a bedroom or she might have dreamed murder rather than sobbing flight. If a dream could hurt like this what might a living woman do to her? She had no claim on James. No right at all to be jealous. Any sign of possessiveness and he would drop her so fast that even Ben would be satisfied.

Those were real tears on her face. She mopped them with a tissue—the dream was surely a warning that she could make such a fool of herself. She had to remember that and guard against giving too much or showing too much. But when she was caught unawares it wasn't easy.

Next day she cooked lunch for Ben and a couple of friends, and during the afternoon a few people strolled in. She was standing at the end of the platform, arms folded, looking out over the fields and seeing nothing in particular, when her shoulder was tapped and James said, 'Waiting for Topham?'

Delight whooshed through her, almost taking her off her feet, so that she did a couple of startled skips and started laughing. 'Whatever are you doing here?

'Driving back. Do you want a lift?'

She had planned to catch a morning train tomorrow, but of course this would be easier. And she didn't really want another evening with Ben's pals and she very much wanted to go with James. She asked, 'Have you seen Ben?'

'He's seen me. I think he was clinching a sale.'

'I'll have a word with him.' This had to be handled carefully, and she hurried to catch Ben, who was just coming out of the showrooms.

'What's he want?' Ben growled.

'He wants to know if I want a lift back.'

'I told him, I'll run you back myself in the morning.'

'That's stupid. It's a long way for you and I might as well go now. If I don't it will seem odd for the sake of another hour or two.' James had reached them and she said, 'I'll get my bag.'

Packing only took a matter of minutes. When she came back the men were more or less where she had left them. James was looking at a picture and Ben was watching him sullenly. Ben was very uptight, and Rosalyn said brightly, 'This will be better than staying till tomorrow. There's a rehearsal in the morning and I should be there. It's a new play next week. Only another six days for Becky.'

'Only on stage,' James said and Rosalyn laughed.

Ben put a stop to that, enquiring with studied insolence, 'Nothing I can show you in here, of course? Having seen your place, I realise there'd be nothing here worth your while.'

Rosalyn kissed her brother's cheek and babbled, 'It's been lovely being here. You take care of yourself,' and led the way out before Ben could say any more.

James took her bag and opened the car door for her, and Ben mouthed at her, 'Remember what I said.'

'Don't worry,' she said softly.

'And remember me to Jeremy,' Ben said loudly as James got into the driving-seat.

She waved to her brother as long as she could see him but he didn't wave back.

'How's trade?' James enquired, and she said automatically,

'Oh, fine.'

'Suddenly your brother seems to have a chip the size of an oak tree on his shoulder.'

She could hardly say, Because somebody told him you have the reputation of a rattlesnake. Instead she admitted, 'Well, times are tough.'

'Remember him to Jeremy.' That had been said for his benefit. 'Does he think you and Jeremy have a future together?'

'He hoped so. He likes Jeremy.'

'Which doesn't surprise me.' The irony was blatant. Jeremy was likeable but he was also rich. It was the money that made him a brother-in-law Ben could take to and James knew that. When she stayed silent he said, 'I hope you told him that Charles and Hilary will always be grateful to you for saving Jeremy's life but they'll never accept you as a daughter. And that they hold the purse-strings.'

He still wasn't blaming them. He still didn't think she was good enough for Jeremy, and she said coldly, 'That's your opinion, is it?'

'My opinion is what it's always been. You'd drive the poor devil out of his mind.'

There were no market stalls in town today. She looked out on mostly closed shops and drawled, 'That might be fun for him.'

'It wouldn't be. Nor for you.' She turned, scowling, and he said, 'Don't sulk. It's the truth.'

'I don't sulk,' she snapped.

'Your brother does, so there's one difference between you.'

They had just left a very surly Ben so all she could say to that was, 'Oh, do shut up.'

'And don't be childish.' The long mouth quirked. 'I didn't go out of my way to pick you up to quarrel with you.'

'And what do you propose doing with me?' Her tone was tart but the query had a suggestiveness she hadn't intended, and when he began to laugh she had to smile.

'I wanted your company,' he said. 'Let's leave Jeremy and Ben out of it.'

She didn't want to quarrel. She didn't even want to argue because he was right; she and Jeremy were wrong for each other. So she was just going to enjoy the next few hours having James all to herself.

He had said she could drive a man wild. Jeremy, he

meant, not himself, but that was admitting she had witchery in her and she could feel the magic now, tingling in her blood as though all the danger and excitement she had found in her acting were in this man.

'Tell me about next week's production,' he said, and she played it for him, describing the scenes and the other roles, giving her lines the full treatment. At the end he said, 'You're going to be sensational.'

She blushed with pleasure. 'Do you really think so?'

'I do.' And it was as if she had just auditioned for the role of a lifetime and got it. She trusted his judgement. She trusted him. It was an instinctive certainty, a gut reaction, but she was beginning to believe that if James was rooting for her life would be good to her.

She talked about her weekend, and when she named the folk she had met she waited for him to say, 'I've had dealings with him.' Or even for a change of expression that could mean that. But she could have been telling him about strangers as she chattered on.

'Did your business go well?' she asked at last.

'It could hardly fail. It was an out-of-court settlement.' His client had obviously done nicely but he was not discussing the case and he changed the subject. 'I had intended to come back yesterday but I decided to stay on.' She would have been fascinated to hear who with, but he was not telling that either. 'I tried to ring you several times on Friday night. The last time you were—sleeping.'

He knew, of course, that Ben had censored his call, and she bit her lip because it had been so stupid. Ben stood no chance of blocking James. He didn't carry the weight, physically or mentally.

'We went to the local for a meal,' she said. 'I told you, where there were all these people.' She was used to crowds but Friday's mob had seemed noisy and instrusive, so that she had longed for peace and quiet.

She had that now. There was music playing very softly. She didn't recognise it. It was probably classical and her musical education and tastes were for today's numbers. She asked, 'What is it?'

'Mendelssohn. "Andante" from one of the concertos. Do you like it?'

'Yes. I don't know much about this kind of music. Perhaps I should listen and learn.'

He smiled at her, 'Shouldn't we all?' he said. He listened far more than he talked, listened and learned, and the music was beautiful. She half closed her eyes and let it flow over her, and wondered how much of this blissful feeling was due to the music and how much to the man.

She thought, I can be quiet with you. Even when the music stops, a word, a look, a smile could be enough. And when he looked at her now his smile seemed to enfold her like the music, as though he had put his arms around her. Although with his hands on the wheel he obviously did nothing of the sort.

With shadows of night falling she said, 'We're going to be rather late and they're not expecting me till tomorrow. Should I phone?'

'It might be a good idea.' Ten minutes later he drew up in the forecourt of a small hotel. 'There'll be a phone here.'

Waterside Inn probably backed on to a river. In the

foyer the fragrance of cherry logs on an open fire greeted them, and now they were here it was a pleasant break and the seafood menu was tempting.

They ate trout with almonds with a glass of wine, in a bright little dining-room from which a staircase rose to a first-floor landing. There were others around but space enough for privacy, and it was so different from the last time Rosalyn had faced James over a restaurant table.

This was cosy, intimate, and—happy was the word. She was really happy, chattering away again, telling him about Roddy and Lou because he had asked how long she was staying at the Hiatts'. 'They could have another bust-up any day and then she'll put him out or he'll take himself off, but I'd rather not be there for the build-up. They throw things. They scream at each other.'

'"The course of true love never did run smooth,"' he quoted, and she hooted.

'True love has nothing to do with it.'

'Now what makes you think, that?'

Because it was all done for effect. Roddy and Lou were always upstaging each other. She smiled, shaking her head. 'They're acting all the time. They don't mean any of it. It's a game.'

'And how would you know?' He was giving her her cues, helping the story along, and she said what the whole company knew.

'If either of them got the break, into films or TV or anything for a wider audience, he or she would be off at a rate of knots and wouldn't give a second thought to the one left behind. As you put a part you're not playing any more out of your mind.'

She finished her coffee and set her cup down. It was a pretty floral design and she turned it on the saucer, following the pattern. 'True love you'd surely go on remembering for a long time,' she mused. 'The pleasure, the pain. Don't you think so?'

She was not speaking from experience; she had never been deeply in love, but she knew very well that Roderick and Louise were not.

'Yes,' he said quietly. 'I think you would remember the pain,' and she recognised the voice of experience, although when she looked up, startled, the smooth-skinned high-boned face was impassive as a mask. 'We should be making that phone call,' he said.

They had finished their meal and they should be on their way. She agreed reluctantly. 'I guess so.'

'There is an alternative. We could stay here. I could book a room.'

She was unprepared, and she was scared. James was asking her to spend the night in his bed, but he wasn't desperate for her. The suggestion of a shared room had been an afterthought. It wouldn't mean very much to him but when she thought what it might do to her her heart began to leap like a trapped rabbit's. She shook her head wordlessly and he said, 'I'll tell them you're on your way.'

She watched him walking between the tables, and she saw how others looked after him, as though he were a celebrity they couldn't quite place. He was much taller than average with a strong and striking face, and there was an assurance even in the way he moved that would always turn heads. He looked a man to be reckoned with, and most of those who glanced at him when he passed followed him with their eyes.

Rosalyn nearly got up too and hurried after him to say, I've changed my mind. She wanted to go with him up that staircase, along the corridor, to open a door on a room, and close the door after them and let everything happen that her body was aching for.

But he hadn't even waited for her to say no. She had shaken her head, but she could have been turning down another cup of coffee for all he had done to persuade her. He seemed neither disappointed nor disconcerted. It had just been a suggestion that they might stay here. If she preferred it they could drive on, no hassle.

She wondered whether she had misheard. He might have said 'book rooms'. Only he hadn't, and there had to be years of experience behind that kind of sophistication. But not a lot of refusals, I'll bet, she thought wryly, and took a quick peek at herself in her handbag mirror.

She managed a touch of lipstick. Then she put on a Becky expression, bland and unfazed, and sat back waiting for him to come back, telling herself how sensible she was being.

The rest of the journey passed quickly. She was bright and funny. She would not for the world have him think she had been knocked out by a proposition. She got them often enough. Tonight's was different because this man was different, but she was comfortable with him still and she was sorry when they reached the drive of the Hiatts' home.

There were lights on in most of the windows—it wasn't that late—and it was a splendid house but she couldn't stay here much longer. She said, 'It's back to Lou and Rod next week. I shall get some earplugs.'

'Make sure you hear what's going on. I don't want you getting hit by any flying objects.'

'I'll watch out for them.' She rolled her eyes, and he smiled.

'That's my Becky,' he said, and she got a queer little flutter in her throat almost as though he had kissed her.

He didn't kiss her. He reached over to open the door for her and went with her to the house door where Hilary was waiting, and said goodnight to them both. And she had to control this impulse to run after him whenever he walked away.

'How's Jeremy?' she asked Jeremy's mother.

'He wants you to look in before he settles down for the night.' Hilary sounded cheerful, and although Jeremy was in bed he grinned happily when the two women walked into his room. Rosalyn crossed to take the hand he was holding out to her, and had to bend to kiss him when he tugged her down. 'I'm glad you're back,' he said. 'I've missed you. I'm glad you didn't stay away till tomorrow.'

His mother frowned very slightly and Rosalyn knew it would not be long before she outwore her welcome here unless her position was made plain. She would be going soon anyway but Jeremy, like Ben, had to accept that the role of Mrs Hiatt Junior had never been on her agenda.

She said, 'Ben said to tell you he tried but I still know best.'

'I can wait.' said Jeremy and he made that sound so heartfelt that it was no wonder his mother sighed.

She stayed, talking to the nurse, when Rosalyn went.

She smiled, brightly enough, and said, 'Sleep well, my dear. I'll see you in the morning.'

From the windows of the guest-room Rosalyn looked over at the lights in James's apartment.

'You're right again,' she said. 'They still don't want me for a daughter.' She opened her bag and took out her things, talking to herself as she wandered round, hanging up clothes, putting toiletries and cosmetics in place. 'That's not to say I'm not wanted. Jeremy, poor lamb, still thinks he wants me, and so did you tonight, didn't you? Not a lot. Not enough to do any urging, but the offer was made.'

In the bathroom she dropped toothbrush and tooth-paste into a tumbler, and told her reflection in the mirrored walls, 'I don't think that was for Jeremy, to finally fix things there, but I think it might have been because of the memories.'

She had brought some woman out of his past, by babbling about true love. And if she had said yes she might have helped to ease the pain and get him through the night. He had been good company for the rest of the journey, relaxed and witty, self-possessed as ever, but now he was alone was he remembering?

Perhaps playing music they had shared. No, he was no masochist. Although he might be sitting in one of those dark brown leather armchairs, downing a brandy to blur the pain and the memories of a dead love.

Or a dead lover? When that chilling thought came she wished she could say, However you lost her, I wish I could help you, because I think that I love you.

She went back into the bedroom, across the window, and said, 'Next time I'll stay.' She pulled the curtains together although no one could see into here, and stood with her back to them and her arms wrapped around herself. There was bound to be another chance, and next time she would take it because she was so obsessed by the man that he was already under her skin, inside her.

But she didn't get the chance for a while.

When Sally brought in her breakfast tray next morning Rosalyn was dressed and waiting to take it from her. Those three days had made all the difference; she felt much stronger and healthier, and she drank some coffee and then carried her tray along to Jeremy's room to finish her breakfast with him.

'How are you?' she asked him, and he said ruefully,

'They tell me I'm getting better, but it's still hell to breathe and I've still got these bloody headaches. No need to ask how you are.'

She felt a little guilty for breezing in beaming, and she sobered hastily. 'Well, nothing much happened to me, did it? And I've more or less had a week off to get over it.'

'You must take me to see this old railway station,' said Jeremy.

She replied, 'Sure I will. It's a gem. Talking of trains, James was telling me he'd been on the Orient Express. You didn't go with him, I suppose?' She knew darn well he hadn't and he gave her a name without any more prompting.

'No, that was Penelope.' And some information she could have done without. 'She's a stunner.'

Of course she was. Does she wear diamonds in her hair? Rosalyn might have asked and Jeremy would have said, Does she *what*?

'Is she still around?' Rosalyn smiled and sipped her orange juice.

'Oh, yes.' So Penelope was not the lost love.

'Is it serious?'

Jeremy grinned. 'I wouldn't know, but James is in London all this week and that's Penelope's home ground, so who knows?'

'That's nice,' said Rosalyn. 'I have to be at the theatre for a rehearsal by ten. Anything I can get you in town?'

All Jeremy's material needs were being met, of course; he needed no one to go shopping for him, and he wanted her back here as soon as the rehearsal was over.

She finished her own breakfast, coaxing him into eating his and chatting about all manner of things with Jeremy, and with Nurse, who was pleased to see her again because she brightened up the patient. Left to himself young Mr Hiatt was inclined to feel sorry for himself, and in Nurse's opinion Mother was a born fusser.

Hilary arrived in the room as Rosalyn was leaving and offered to run her to the theatre.

'Thank you,' Rosalyn said, 'but I've got plenty of time to walk and I need the exercise.'

'You won't go off with any of them? You will come right back?' Jeremy pleaded anxiously, and Hilary tutted.

'Rosalyn is an *actress*. She *has* to be at the theatre. The show must go on.'

'Now where have I heard that before?' Rosalyn muttered under her breath, and set off, striding out,

getting away from the Hiatts' house and James's apartment. He could be gone already and how she had
gulped down that breakfast she did not know. Her
head still seemed to be ringing, as if she had been
slapped hard on either cheek.

She wouldn't be seeing James for days. She would
have to leave 'next door' before he came back and it
was always possible that he wouldn't bother to seek
her out again. And while he was away he would be on
Penelope's home ground. Penelope, who was a stunner
and about whom he could be serious. By the time she
reached the theatre Rosalyn was in just the mood to
play a thoroughly unpleasant character.

But the rehearsal went well, they all seemed glad to
see her and her spirits lifted. James would come back
and if he didn't contact her she would get in touch with
him, and of course there were Penelopes but the firm
had a London office and that was where James would
be heading.

Meanwhile she was sorry she had more or less
promised to rush away after the rehearsal, and she
walked slowly back to the Hiatts' after a sandwiches
and coffee break with Lou and two other girls on the
grass outside the theatre on the Green.

Jeremy was downstairs, sitting with cushioned support and feet up on the sofa in the drawing-room, and
his mother opened the front door just before Rosalyn
reached it as if she had been on the look-out for her.

Hilary was enquiring how the rehearsal had gone,
but Jeremy cut across her words as the women walked
into the room, asking Rosalyn, 'Can you get off for a
few more days next week?'

'Of course I can't.' Rosalyn laughed at the very idea and Hilary took over.

'We're going to stay with friends who have a house in Wales. It's by the sea and the doctors think it can only do Jeremy good. Nurse is coming with us, but we do understand that have your work to do. After all you are the star of that sweet little theatre, aren't you? The show——'

'Must go on,' Rosalyn completed it for her. 'Oh, it must, and so must I. But what a good idea—it will be lovely for you by the sea at this time of year.'

Jeremy was unconvinced about that; nor, he complained, did he feel up to the journey. But his mother was even more used to getting her own way than he was. Jeremy had been passed fit to travel in limousine luxury and both she and his father were badly in need of a break.

'It will do you all good, of course it will,' said Rosalyn. And a change of scene might, but his parents were really getting him away because they still believed she was intent on nabbing their boy.

'I shall phone you every day,' Jeremy vowed passionately, and his mother looked as if this rescue operation had not been planned a moment too soon.

After the big house the flat seemed claustrophic, but Roddy and Lou were being careful, probably because Rosalyn might have pointed out that her name was on the rent-book, not his. As it was the atmosphere was easy going and they were keeping histrionics for the stage. She hardly missed the high-living standards of the Hiatts and she didn't miss Jeremy at all.

Lou, of course, was intrigued about the situation

with Jeremy. 'Absolutely nothing is going on,' Rosalyn said emphatically.

'But what about James Halloran?

They had all asked her that when she'd turned up for rehearsal on Monday and she had said, 'He was at the theatre with Jeremy's mother. He's a friend of the family.'

As soon as she got her alone Louise asked her again, Rosalyn repeated herself and Louise drooled, 'I could go for him in a very big way.'

This time Rosalyn added, 'You'd be wasting your time. He's heavily involved with some girl called Penelope; he's with her this week.' That made Louise sigh and give up, but as she listened to herself Rosalyn knew she didn't believe a word she was saying.

Jeremy rang every evening, late, when the show was over, and she chatted with him, trying to jolly him along. She was glad it needed be no longer than a few minutes because these days Jeremy seemed to do nothing but moan.

Ben rang her too, on Thursday afternoon, and he sounded as gloomy as Jeremy. He had tried to get her at the Hiatts' and, 'A girl told me you were here. Have you walked out on him?'

'I didn't need to,' she said. 'Because his people have taken him off to keep him away from me. They'd disinherit him sooner than let him marry me, so the question never really did arise. That was probably Sally you spoke to. The family have hit the trail and left it all to the maid and the housekeeper.'

Lou and Rod came in with a carrier-bag of groceries while Ben was still insisting that she had missed a golden opportunity there. 'Yeah, yeah,' she said.

'Look, I'll ring you later. This must be costing a fortune at this time.'

She rang him the following night from a call-box in the theatre and by then he seemed to have cheered up. 'Seen much of Halloran?' he asked her, and she said,

'I've seen nothing of him,' which was what Ben wanted to hear.

James did not phone. She had thought he might, and all that week whenever a phone rang near her it brought a fleeting hope. But then, on Saturday, the flowers were delivered.

They were in the dressing-room when she arrived to get into Becky's costume for the last time. 'Like old times, isn't it?' said Kimberley wistfully. Jeremy's floral displays had been a regular weekly feature for months. Now Rosalyn was back in the theatre here were the flowers again, and the card signed 'J'.

Lou read the message aloud. '"Tread softly, Becky." What's he mean by that?'

'Go carefully, I suppose,' said Rosalyn. 'Mind what you're doing.'

The flowers were freesias, which might be a coincidence and nothing to do with the Orient Express. They could have come from Jeremy, but he had never called her Becky. It had to be James, and was, maybe, a disarming way of telling her to behave herself.

She got a jug from Props and put them in water, and she slipped the card into her purse. She had never carried Jeremy's sentimental notes around, but this was different, whatever the message meant. And there was that line in the poem by Yeats, 'Tread softly because you tread on my dreams.'

James was not a dreamer but the Orient Express had

been a daydream. She took the flowers back to the flat with her that night, and when Jeremy rang he never mentioned them. 'Can you come down tomorrow?' he wanted to know. 'Stay overnight and——'

'No,' she said promptly. 'I've got a million things to do.'

She had plenty to keep her busy on Sunday but the main thing she was doing, right until the curtain was due to rise on the first night of the new play on Monday, was waiting for James.

She had stopped waiting a couple of minutes before, when she peered through the curtain and saw him in the audience. After that she gave the performance of her life. She would have played her part well in almost any circumstances, but tonight she was inspired.

The play was a murder mystery and she was the smiling villain. Watching her, the playwright, a young local man whose first production this was, could hardly believe the thrilling, chilling character he had created. 'Lady Macbeth rides again,' said the producer in the interval. 'Great stuff, sweetie.'

When she took her bows this time James was applauding, and she smiled across the footlights at him and said, without words, I'll be right with you.

She was off stage and into the dressing-room like a whirlwind, stripping off costume and make-up without wasting a second. 'Aren't you the deep one?' said Lou, and Rosalyn grinned at her

'Whatever do you mean?'

'Where or who are you rushing off to?' Margie asked, as Rosalyn collided with her in the corridor.

Rosalyn called, 'Sorry' over her shoulder, hardly checking her pace. As she came out of the stage door

James opened the car door and she reached him, laughing. 'You did come to my first night. Thank you.'

'I wouldn't have missed if for the world,' he said. 'Let's go, before your fans mob you.'

There was no danger of that, although some admirers would have found her if she had stayed there. Jumping into the car and being driven away fast was just a joke, but it was terrific to flop back with James beside her, in control of everything.

When the adrenalin her performance had psyched up ebbed away she could be left utterly drained. Having friends around, even men like Jeremy who thought they loved her, had never helped much. But tonight she was drawing strength from this man. Brushing against his sleeve, she felt again as if he were putting his arms around her. As he would. She knew that. She turned her head, resting her cheek on the seat back, watching him. 'It did go well, didn't it?' she said.

'It went very well.' She loved his deep voice that could send shivers of delight up and down her spine.

'Did you send me the flowers?' she asked.

'Of course.'

Yes, of course. Later she would ask about the message, and she ran over the lines in her head. . .

I have spread my dreams under your feet;
Tread softly because you tread on my dreams. . .

This was what was happening to her. For the first time real life was more thrilling than dreams. They were taking the road to the better end of town, and she asked, 'Where are we going?'

'My place?' He made it a question and she laughed softly.

'I can hardly invite you to mine. Mine is very crowded.'

'How are the star-crossed lovers?'

'Peace reigns,' she said gaily. 'Nothing being chucked around so far.'

'So you don't want to leave the flat to them?'

'Chance would be a fine thing. Do you know of any cheap lodgings?'

'Possibly.' And he might well, although his idea of a reasonable rent could differ from hers.

'I'd be interested,' she said.

There were few lights on in the Hiatts' house. The family were not back yet and when Jeremy rang the flat tonight they could tell him that Rosalyn had gone with James. It didn't matter; he would have to be told. But it was going to depress him even more and she sighed.

'What's the matter?' James asked.

'Not a thing,' she said very brightly. 'What could be the matter?'

They parked the car in the basement garage and took the lift to the penthouse flat. Last time she was in here he had kissed her, and she had got out as if the place was on fire. This time she would go up in flames, and she found herself staring blindly at a painting, panic beginning to build up inside her.

When he turned her towards him she put flat hands on his chest and her voice came out in a squeak. 'You did like the play?'

'We're talking about your performance, aren't we?'

She was not fishing for compliments. She hardly

knew what she was talking about, she was so nervous. 'I thought you might just be comedy, melodrama,' he said, 'but you're better than that.'

'It was a good part,' she mumbled and he contradicted her.

'No. Nor was it a good play, but you made it one.'

He was proud of her and that was wonderful, and maybe she would always be better than her best if he was near. As an actress. As a lover, although there she was a novice among some brilliant competition. Once he had her he might stop wanting her. Don't call us, we'll call you.

'Let me show you round,' he said. He could afford to be patient. He had time on his side as well as all that experience. They both knew she was here for the night but as she walked around with him she began to feel at home.

She ran fingertips along an ormolu and marquetry side-cabinet, held a tiny jade figure, looked at first editions on the bookshelves and a modern painting by a so far unknown artist.

She went into a super kitchen and asked, 'Does it get much use?'

He said, 'From time to time.' The study was always in use, you could see that, although all the papers on the big desk appeared to be in order.

When he opened another door she said, 'Lovely.' There was a good-sized single bed, the furniture fitted, the floor deeply carpeted.

'Would you consider this reasonable lodgings?' he said.

He was asking her to move in. That meant he had never thought of her as a one-night stand. It was almost a commitment, and she was going to take it just as soon as she was sure he was serious. She smiled as she asked, 'How much?'

'A peppercorn rent.' He was not smiling. He was waiting as if what she said next could be of the utmost importance, and she felt as if she were riding a shooting star, dizzy and light-headed.

She knew that he could be everything for her and if she had him she could do anything. She could make him forget Penelope; hold back the pain in his past. She said, 'I'm sure I could manage a peppercorn.'

In the study the phone rang. 'Let it ring,' he said, and because nothing could spoil things now she began to laugh.

'It can't be for me and it can't be any of my business, but I can't let a phone ring without answering it. I don't know a woman who can.'

'Those earplugs you were talking about,' he said. 'If you bought them, bring them along.'

She followed him and stood just outside the room as he picked up the phone from the desk. And she knew then that she should have let it ring because he said, 'Have you called the police? Well, do that and don't touch anything; I'll be right with you.'

She gulped. 'A client?'

'A break-in, at the Hiatts'.' He strode past her. 'You stay here.'

He had gone before she could get her breath back, and it was an awful shock. That sort of thing was always happening but when it happened to you, or to those you knew well, it really hit you and it was sickening. The place was burglar-alarmed but every big house was and that didn't seem to stop them. Poor Mrs

Beddows must be going out of her mind. She was probably the one who had phoned here, even before she called the police, so that showed the state she was in.

'Oh, Lord!' Rosalyn whispered, remembering the pictures and all the treasures that Hilary and Charles had gathered around them. Jeremy's accident had been blow enough and now this. It was unfair, wicked; life could be horrible, and she couldn't stay here. She couldn't do anything, but she had to go round and find out what was happening.

She pulled the door so that it locked behind her, ran down the stairs and walked quickly down the drive and up towards the Georgian house. There were no cars here yet—the police would be coming soon, but all the lights seemed to be on now, and the front door was open.

As she walked into the hall James barred her way. Before she had taken more than a couple of paces he had grabbed her arm and was hustling her out of the house, and she looked back fearfully, dreading what he might be hiding from her.

When he spoke his voice was grim. 'I told you to stay.'

'What's happened?' she faltered. 'Is anyone hurt?'

'No. Get out of here.'

'All right, I'm sorry I came. I might not be much help but I am concerned.'

He was walking her towards the road and his grip on her arm made the healing bruises ache. 'Not personally concerned, I trust?' he said, which didn't make any sort of sense.

At the gates he loosed her and looked down at her, and the lines on his face were deep and harsh. 'But if that conman brother of yours is in on this don't even consider giving him an alibi again.'

CHAPTER SEVEN

'WHAT did you say?' Rosalyn croaked, but Halloran didn't need to repeat anything. His expression said it all again as he looked at her. In the still air she could hear the faint siren of a police car, and a woman came hurrying out of the house.

Then he said, 'Go back,' and went to meet the woman, and she knew that she would never again want to follow him anywhere. Her every instinct now was to put miles between them.

She walked past the drive leading to the apartments. She had locked that door behind her. Somebody might have let her in but she would never go back there and, once past, she began to run and kept running until she was into town.

She waited outside a phone-box for someone to finish a call, leaning against a wall practising breathing, in-out, in-out, and when she had the receiver in her hand she remembered that she had no purse and no money and had to make it a reversed charge.

After a while she was told there was no reply, so she would have to keep walking around and phoning until Ben did answer. She had to speak to him and she couldn't go back to her own flat. She couldn't face Lou and Roddy yet. She couldn't face anyone. She couldn't trust anyone.

God knew how long it would be before she could even trust herself when she had been so abysmally

140

wrong about James. He was an iceman. Maybe Ben was a bit of a conman, a wheeler-dealer, but how dared James leap to the conclusion that Ben was involved in the break-in? He had no proof, no reason.

And what did he mean by talking about her 'giving him an alibi again'? The whole thing was crazy. The more she thought about it the weirder it got. She had never given anyone an alibi, but James had sounded as if he suspected that she and Ben were in some sort of plot together.

She was walking round a square where the terraced houses opened on to the pavement, and she glanced through an uncurtained window to where a fire burned in a darkened room. She remembered the fire then.

She had been sharing Ben's digs, using a sofa in the living-room, just finishing drama school, when the works had gone up in an inferno in the dead of night. Everything had been gutted; it had been an electrical fault, an accident. Afterwards there had been questioning and she had backed Ben's claim that he had been home all night. That had been an alibi of sorts, but she had been telling the truth and it had all been years ago.

How could James have heard about it? And even if he had that was no excuse for turning on Ben, and on her, like a prosecuting counsel. She could never forigve him for that.

The rain was so fine that she hardly noticed it, but the coolness was welcome on her burning face as she walked to the next phone-box. The streets were almost empty now. The occasional house lights were in upstairs windows; everyone was going to bed and she was losing her sense of time.

Where *was* Ben? Out, obviously, but the odds were

he would be home before morning and she had to talk to him if she walked the streets all night. Her keys for the flat were back there in her handbag. Lou and Roddy would let her in and then she could say, I've got to make a private phone call. Please go back into your room and shut the door.

Only of course Lou would listen, especially when Rosalyn arrived looking like this. Even misty rain became drenching after a while and by now it was reaching her skin through her clothes. She didn't mind that. She was still burning with fury. A howling storm would have suited her mood, thunder and lightning, so that she could have thrown back her head and screamed into it.

When she finally heard Ben's voice she nearly screamed at him, Where have you *been*? I've been trying to get you for *hours*. But that would have been hysterical and she had to be calm.

'What's up?' he was asking her and she said,

'Something terrible has happened here. There's been a break-in at the Hiatts'. I don't know what's been taken but the art collection's practically priceless, and it's quite awful.' She raised her voice over Ben's shocked exclamations. 'But hold it, that isn't all. That's just the beginning. James thinks you could have had something to do with it.'

'*What*?' Ben yelped. 'Who did he say this to?'

'To me. Just to me. I was in his apartment and someone rang from the house, even before they'd phoned the police, and he went round and when I followed him he shoved me out of the house, and that was when he said it, "If that conman brother of yours is in on this," he said, "don't even consider giving him an alibi again."'

'What——?' Ben began and she rushed on,

'No, I don't know what he meant. I've been walking round town ever since trying to phone you. All I can think is maybe it's something to do with the fire insurance from the old paint-stripping business, but that was years ago.'

'Has he talked to the police?'

'I don't know. I suppose so. And I don't know why he's got it in for you. What were you told about him?'

'He made me edgy, so I asked around and what I heard was it he'd got it in for you you might as well cut your throat.'

Her blood ran cold, but nothing could be that bad. She forced herself to sound reasonable. 'Take it easy. It's an awful thing altogether, but you've got nothing to do with it, so nobody can do anything to you. And if he did accuse you to anyone else you could sue him for libel or slander or whatever.'

'Sue Halloran?' Ben snorted. 'Be your age.' There was silence for a few seconds then he said, 'You've got to talk to him. He must fancy you or he wouldn't be ferrying you all over the country. I don't want the authorities down here. They wouldn't find the Hiatt haul but you can bet they'd find something. Half the stuff you get in this business you don't know where it's come from, and it isn't all junk I've got. Some of it's under wraps.

'Go and tell him he's wrong. I've been in some dodgy deals but this time I'm in the clear. Ask him to leave me out of it. For your sake. Tell him how much we mean to each other.'

She couldn't go crawling and pleading. She said dully, 'He's not going to do anything because I ask him.'

'Ring me back. Go and get him now. Get him on his own and offer him anything.'

Herself, he meant. What else had she got to offer? Again she said, 'I'm not that good an actesss,' but this time it didn't shame Ben. This time he said, almost savagely,

'Sister, you had better be,' and she was left with a dead phone in her hand.

When she put down the phone she was shivering. Trying to steer her into a marriage bed was one thing; telling her to seduce James Halloran was something else entirely. She walked from the phone box still shaking, and she couldn't have said if that was shock or because, 'He must fancy you. . .offer him anything,' was the sickest joke she had ever heard.

Ben must be out of his mind. She couldn't do it and it wouldn't work. James had stopped fancying her. She had nothing to offer that he wanted and she didn't believe he had a price. He was probably the most incorruptible man she had ever met, but she had to do something.

She had phoned Ben to warn him. Not because she thought for a moment that he was in on the break-in, but because she couldn't know everything he was up to; his storeroom was kept locked and he always had been a chancer. Dodgy deals might not frighten him but James Halloran seemed to scare him silly.

Anyhow, she had to get her handbag back sometime, and she needed her key to get into the flat and out of the rain. She went on walking, trying to block out the confusion in her mind. She could do that in the theatre before the curtain rose, but it was harder with the rain on her face, fighting this hollow feeling of a double betrayal. First James and now Ben.

The lights were on in Halloran's apartment. That didn't mean he was there—they had been on when she let herself out—but she pressed the bell and spoke into the grille. 'It's Rosalyn.'

'Come up,' he said. If he was not alone she would just collect her handbag and leave everything until tomorrow. Ben would have to wait. She could hardly bring up his name if the place was full of policemen.

The lights in the hall and on the stairs were muted, but she saw James waiting at the top of the stairs as she dragged herself up, step by step. From a long way off his dark and heavy shadow seemed to fall on her.

Inside the apartment he said, 'Sit down,' and she longed for the strength to say, I'll stand, but by then her legs were so rubbery that she went down into the nearest chair just in time.

There was no one else in the room. It was well after midnight but he was still dressed as she had seen him last. 'What have you been doing?' he asked.

She probably looked as if she had come out of the river. She said, 'I've been walking, and trying to make sense out of what you said. It was a terrible thing to say. Of course Ben had nothing to do with it.'

He sat down too, in the brown winged-back armchair, watching her with hooded eyes and that formidable stillness of his. 'He told you that?'

'Yes.'

'Did he suggest you came round here and told me?'

'Yes.'

'Using, no doubt, your not inconsiderable charm.' The sardonic hint of a smile that went with that brought the colour flaming to her face so that she might as well have admitted Yes again. 'A very caring brother,' he drawled. It *had* been out of character for Ben to try to use her this way but he had seemed desperate.

'Offer him anything,' Ben had said. He hadn't said, Deliver. He probably meant charm and cheat, and a fat chance she had of doing either.

She said earnestly, 'My brother is not a crook. You called him a conman—well, maybe he is in a very small way. He's street-smart; he's had to be. Come to that, so am I.'

'Exactly.'

She wasn't sure where he was agreeing with her. She stared at him and he said, 'Your record proved that.'

'*My* record? I don't have a record.'

'Not in the legal sense,' he said drily, 'but it was enough to make the Hiatts anxious to keep Jeremy out of your clutches.

'They had me investigated?'

'Yes.'

If she had been standing that could have floored her. It sent her back in her chair and she croaked, 'Did Jeremy know?'

'No.'

'But you did?'

'Yes.'

'And you thought that was all right, did you?' Biting scorn edged her words. 'I cannot imagine what was dished up for them because I can't recall much happening to me that's worth a mention. Did it occur to you that it could have been a load of lies?'

'Not from the man we used,' he said quietly and she leapt on that.

'*We* used? You?'

'Yes.'

She gave a little trill of mocking laughter. 'Maybe I should be selling it to the papers if it's that hot. Do you have a copy handy?'

'Yes.'

She played it like Becky, simpering, 'I would be vastly obliged if you would allow me to peruse it,' and he brought a thin folder from a drawer in the desk in the study.

It turned her to stone almost from the first word. It began at the beginning, and Rosalyn Becket's background would not have impressed anybody. A slum child with a drunken father, and he *did* have a record. She was surprised Aunt Eleanor had never mentioned that, although she had nagged interminably about 'Your no-good father and your mother God-rest-her who was no better than she should have been'.

That would probably have been enough for a snob like Hilary, and during the years Rosalyn had lived with her mother's sister there had been social workers after Rosalyn had tried to run away. She had been trying to get to Ben, but that had never come out. A wild child, a rebel, not a reassuring juvenile record.

The fire at the paint-stripping works was an item: her evidence on behalf of her brother, and 'arson suspected'.

From then on she was a young working actress, and it all sounded single-minded and ambitious. Her breaks had come through hard work and talent, but no one could prove they were not for favours.

Emotional involvements, where she had walked away from commitments. It could have been the CV of a hard-as-nails little grabber and she drawled, 'I can see why they didn't want me in the family. But you need not have bothered, because wild horses wouldn't have dragged me in. And after this I only hope I don't have to see any of them again.'

'You must blame me,' he said heavily, and she flared, 'Oh, I do.'

'That insurance claim,' he said. 'The claims investigator is a friend of mine and he was convinced there was arson and fraud and you and your brother were in it together. He said at the time that you were probably the best actesss he'd ever come up against. When Jeremy became infatuated with you his parents were worried.' He smiled without humour. 'And because I was biased against women who carry on like Becky Sharp I had you investigated for them.'

She looked at him with loathing. 'Are you enjoying this?'

'Lord, *no*,' he said harshly, 'I never wanted you to know about the investigation. As far as I'm concerned there's nothing here that matters.' The folder slipped from her hands and lay at her feet. 'I'd give a great deal for this not to be happening,' he said, 'but it has happened, and so we come to your brother.'

She supposed the room was warm but her wet shirt stuck clammily to her skin as the implacable voice went on, 'You may think he's just a Jack-the-lad, but he's a crooked dealer, he's a fence, he's in with professional villains and this job has the marks of insider information.'

Her tongue wouldn't leave the roof of her mouth but

she managed to get out, 'Like what? Ben was only in the house for an hour or two.'

'Long enough to see enough. The alarm was fixed and the canvasses were expertly removed, on the one night for years that the house has been empty. You knew that?'

She knew that Mrs Beddows had been nervous about staying there alone. On Sunday she had gone to fetch her sister. They must have returned last night. Jeremy had told Rosalyn, and she nodded. 'Did you tell Ben?' James asked.

She remembered Lou and Roddy coming into the flat and hearing her say that the family were away. Later she could have told Ben about Sunday; she honestly couldn't remember. She said, 'I don't think so, but he wouldn't be such a fool.'

James said, 'He is a fool,' and she was on her feet, hands over her ears.

'I am not going to listen to this. It's all coincidence and prejudice. Hundreds of people know about the paintings. That picture in the paper of Jeremy and me showed the Matisse and went on about the fabulous house. You can forget Ben. Ben had nothing to do with this.'

He waited as if her outburst might not be quite over, then he asked, 'So what are you going to do?'

She grabbed up a bowl, eggshell fragile and translucent as mother-of-pearl, a single splash of gold its only decoration and shrieked, 'What I would really like to do is smash something that matters to you, seeing how you're trying to spoil everything for me. But it will have to be a possession because folk don't rate with you, do they?'

For a moment she held the bowl high while he sat as unmoved as if he were watching a play, and of course she couldn't smash it. She should have picked on something that was less beautiful, and destroying anything would have been stupid.

She put down the bowl, her back to him, and scooped up her handbag from the table where she had dropped it a lifetime ago.

'Where are you going?' He sounded almost bored.

'Home,' she said. 'You're surely not still offering me cheap lodgings?'

'You could do worse.'

She bit off each word. 'No, I could not.'

'I'll run you back.' He was up and coming towards her, and she backed off, glaring.

'Don't come near me.'

'If you insist on walking I shall follow you. You're in no state to be on the streets alone this time of night.'

'Try it and I'll scream my head off.'

Suddenly he looked weary. 'Don't be ridiculous,' he said, and the fire went out of her. She was wasting her strength carrying on like this. In the circumstances courtesy was crazy, but if he was determined to drive her home she couldn't have a physical tussle with him. She shrugged and went silently beside him, down to the car.

She got in without a word, and sat as far away as she could get, as if his touch would burn her. And when they drew up in front of the house she had her door open before the car had stopped. She was out when he turned and she said, 'I hope you hit a tree.'

'Goodnight,' he said.

The house was asleep. Every window was dark. She

got her key in the front door lock by the light of the street-lamp and felt her way up the stairs. Her eyes were almost accustomed to the dark as she picked up the phone in the living-room and carried it to the window.

By the lamplight she dialled Ben's number again and he answered at once. 'Rosalyn?' He must have been waiting all this time.

'Yes.' She sat hunched over the phone. 'He's got a file on me and on you, I think. The insurance business started it. He knew the claims man; he thought it was fraud, and Hilary and Charles panicked when Jeremy said he was going to marry me. Ben? Are you there?'

'Go on,' said Ben.

'Somebody knew what was in that house. Somebody knew the house was empty. He says you're in with some thieving experts. He must have been keeping tabs on you. They're going to be asking you questions and there's nothing I can do to stop that so you had better get your act together.'

'Right,' and then with a queer little bark of laughter, 'Ah, well, you can't win 'em all,' but before she could ask what he had meant by that the phone clicked and, without warning, light flooded the room.

Lou was standing in her bedroom doorway, her hand on the light switch. 'I thought I heard you,' she said, and her eyes took in Rosalyn's dishevelment, the way she was huddled in the window-seat. 'What are you *doing*?'

'I wish I knew,' Rosalyn said.

Lou shut the door and came to sit beside her. 'Rod's asleep. You look awful—you never walked back? Did you have a row with him?'

Rosalyn drew a deep breath and said, 'Make us a cup of tea, there's a love,' and in the time it took Lou to fill a kettle and switch it on she had pulled herself together just enough to launch into an account of the break-in at the Hiatts', which was drama enough, heaven knew.

She didn't mention Ben. She said that James had just brought her back, they both drank the tea and Rosalyn tried to deal with Lou's eager questioning.

In bed, a little later, she could hear through the thin wall the shocked murmurs of Lou and Roddy discussing the news. And she thought how much shriller and more excited they would be if they had known that James suspected Ben, and that, lying in the darkness, Rosalyn was beginning to have terrible doubts herself.

She hadn't expected to sleep but in the end exhaustion claimed her, and she slept heavily for a few hours. But the moment she woke the nightmare was waiting. How could she doubt Ben when she had loved and trusted him all her life? But now she seemed to be floundering in quicksands where nothing was sure or stable. She got out of bed and stumbled to the bathroom, washing and dressing like an automaton.

The phone rang as she passed and she picked it up, forcing herself to lift it to her ear instead of cutting the caller off. Lou came out of her room and waited, listening, and what promised to be the worst day of Rosalyn's life had begun.

Jeremy was on the phone, distraught at the rape of his home and demoralised by his mother's screaming about Rosalyn's and Ben's criminal connections. 'What was she on about? What criminal connections?' he was spluttering. Hilary was under sedation now and the horror of it all had Jeremy almost incoherent.

'It's all in the report,' she said. 'James has a copy. I'm so sorry.'

She put the phone down. Lou was puzzled but her eyes were gleaming. 'Well?' she prompted.

'Jeremy,' said Rosalyn.

'Was he upset?' That was such a daft question that Lou answered herself, 'Well, of course he would be.' The phone rang again and Lou answered that too. 'It's James Halloran.' Her eyes went even brighter and she gave Rosalyn a things-are-looking-up grin.

Rosalyn had to take it. Today she would have to take everything. There could be no turning away. 'Hello,' she said.

He said, 'This is my number,' and she grabbed an envelope and pen, taking the figures down as he spoke. 'I can be contacted from here if you need me.'

She drew a thick cancelling line through the number. She could not imagine why she had bothered to make a note of it, and she said flippantly, 'I always wanted to play Eliza Doolittle and say, "Not bloody likely."'

'And you can stop play-acting.'

She knew this was real. She wasn't kidding herself, but her voice was still light. 'You think I need a lawyer?'

'You need someone to stop you wrecking your life and your career.'

'Well, it won't be you.'

'Believe me, Becky,' he said, 'I am all you've got.'

She slammed down the phone and as soon as she did she knew that of course she needed him. Possibly as a lawyer, certainly as a friend, she needed him desperately. She dialled the number in frantic haste and when he said, 'Yes?' she said,

'Can I come'.

'I'll fetch you,' he said. 'Meanwhile talk to nobody, especially the Press.'

'There's nobody here yet.'

'There will be any minute.'

Margie the PR girl was not going to like this kind of publicity but it would certainly make the headlines. The Press would be on to Rosalyn like a pack of hounds, but she need not face them alone if she could get to James first. She babbled, 'I'll start walking. I'll go down Hilldrop Terrace and wait for you at the bottom of the road.'

She ran into her bedroom for her purse and a jacket, and Lou was wailing, 'Where are you going? What are you doing?'

'Watch this space,' Rosalyn called, although very soon everyone was going to know it was no joke. She was out of sight of the house within a couple of minutes, and the car rounded a corner before she reached the end of the longish road that was Hilldrop Terrace. She had wished an accident on James when he had put her down last night and now she said sheepishly, 'I'm very glad you didn't hit a tree.'

'I decided to wait,' he said. 'You could have had second thoughts.'

She managed a wry grin then she said, 'Ben had nothing to do with the break-in.' Something might have happened to change James's mind. If he agreed with her now the sun would burst through the clouds.

When he said, 'He's gone,' her jaw fell open.

'*Gone*? He can't have gone. I spoke to him again last night when I got in.' James said nothing; his lean hard profile was inscrutable, and she admitted, 'I don't know much about his business. Only what he tells me.' Her throat was so dry that her voice sounded papery. 'He swore he had nothing to do with this, but I told him he was your suspect and to get his act together.'

James said drily, 'Well, he got his act out of town, if not out of the country.'

In all this madness anything was possible, and she whispered fearfully, 'If he talked, just careless talk that somebody picked up, you don't think afterwards they might try to shut him up because he'd know too much?'

'No.' That was prompt and decisive. 'He's not that naïve.'

'*You* said he was a fool.'

'He is. He was bound to be suspected in an art robbery, although it looks as though the chance was too good to miss. He might have bluffed it out but you probably panicked him last night.'

'You panicked him,' she said. 'Some of his friends have heard of you.'

'And I've heard of some of them.'

'Oh, Lord, how awful!' Tears filled her eyes and she jerked her head towards the window, blinking frantically. 'What am I going to do?'

'Carry on as usual.'

She didn't believe that she could. They might not want her at the theatre. She could imagine how the story would run: the art robbery in the house where she had been a guest for the last few weeks, her wheeler-dealer brother missing and wanted. She asked, 'He left everything? Just walked out of Heritage Halt?'

'The place is mortgaged. It could well be a front.'

The Press would love that. It would make a pretty photograph, would the old railway station. Well, the Orient Express wouldn't be calling there again, not even in her dreams.

They were back in the parking basement of the apartments, passing several people who spoke, but just good mornings, and James steered her past them with the same brief greeting. The phone was ringing when he opened the penthouse door. She stood in the middle of the room, completely at a loss. She could only say, 'I *cannot* believe this.'

'Why should you?' he said.

Because the pieces were falling into place like a terrible jigsaw, and she began to pace up and down. 'I never knew my father had a record. I knew he was a drunk who could be violent, but I didn't know he actually went inside for it. I could hope I took after my mother but according to Aunt Eleanor she was a tramp, so there isn't much hope for me, is there?'

He caught her swinging hand, steadying her so that she had to face him. 'The report on Eleanor Ross,' he said, 'was that she was a highly respected lady.'

Rosalyn howled, 'Oh, she was! They didn't come any more respectable. She was like Miss Pinkerton, you know, Miss Pinkerton's Academy?' She quoted Becky's opening line, ' "You took me in because I was useful—there is no question of gratitude between us." She made a little slave of me. She didn't care about me. She never loved anyone.'

'So why take her word about your mother?' he said. 'And if she was right it could have been worse. You wouldn't have wanted to be Eleanor's daughter.' He tilted her chin, surveying her with that quizzical lift of an eyebrow. 'Cheer up, Becky, and don't start dragging your ancestors into this; we've got problems enough with your brother.'

Hearing him say 'we' was almost as comforting as if he had been holding her tight. She was so thankful he was on her side, and she said shakily, 'I couldn't handle this on my own; I could fall apart.'

'I doubt that, and, as I believe I told you before, I know you well.'

She tried to joke. 'And you had the report to prove it.'

'Things that were not in the report. I knew you wouldn't smash the bowl.'

She nearly had. 'It might have slipped. I had the shakes. If it had would you have given up on me?'

'I don't give up so easily.'

'Thank God for that,' she said fervently.

The phone rang and clicked into the answering machine. Any time now someone would be at the front door, or even reach this door. Soon the outside world would be breaking in. 'Tell me what to do,' she said.

'Let's get some coffee.' He went into the kitchen and she found herself sitting at the table, slicing an apple and spreading butter on toast. She could almost pretend there had been no phone call from the Hiatts and she had stayed here last night and everything was wonderful. No, she couldn't. She didn't think she would ever be able to make believe again.

As he sat down facing her, she asked, 'What did they take?'

'The best of the pictures: the Matisse, a couple of Monets, the Sisley, the Stubbs.'

'Ben liked the Stubbs.' She could taste nausea, as she had when she'd nearly fainted on stage. She said wildly, 'And how about the candlesticks in the window-alcove upstairs? One of those has his fingerprints on. He picked that up, checking the hallmark very likely. I suppose they'll be testing for fingerprints.'

'For elimination purposes. Yours, mine, family and friends.' He grinned. 'You can imagine how that will go down with Hilary.' If she started giggling it could end in the screaming habdabs, so she bit her lip and muttered,

'I will never be forgiven.'

'Probably not, but you can live with it.' He brushed that aside as no problem at all. 'Finish your coffee and we'll go and have a chat with the man in charge.'

'The police?'

'Them first and then the Press.'

The man into whose office they were ushered at the local station was tall and thin with a nose slightly off-centre, as if it had been broken some time, giving him a sinister air. He obviously knew James, and greeted him as if they got on well together. And he thanked Rosalyn for coming in, although she knew she would soon have been contacted if she had not.

A policewoman was sitting at a table and another man was by a filing cabinet. Rosalyn was given a chair. James sat sideways, watching her as she faced Detective Inspector Murray, and it was a comfort that James was not only the biggest man in the room but one of the smartest lawyers going. He would stop her making a fool of herself, and she sat up straight and answered quietly and clearly.

Yes, she had known the house was empty from

Sunday till Monday. She might have mentioned it to her brother. They would learn that from Lou and Roddy anyway, and the inspector was right down to the nitty-gritty. It was Ben who interested him. Had she any idea where Ben might be?

She said, 'No,' remembering her brother saying that he had contacts abroad. He hadn't told her where. He had never really told her anything.

'When were you last in touch with him?' she was asked.

'I rang him last night and told him what had happened.'

'But you were with him recently?' Did they think her trip to Heritage Halt could have been plotting time?

'I was driving down to the area on business on Friday and I took Miss Becket with me,' James explained. 'We came back together on Sunday.'

The 'together' was helping, distancing her from Ben's circle, emphasising that her link with James was not just lawyer and client, that he was vouching for her as a friend.

When the inspector said that if Ben should get in touch she should let them know it was James who said, 'Of course, but they see very little of each other. Until her recent car crash it was over a year since they'd met. She is the star of our local theatre, as you know, and her career takes up most of her time.'

He stressed her bright prospects, how good her future looked, that she was auditioning next week for a TV play. Was she heck, but it was a sound argument against her risking everything getting mixed up in a house raid practically on her doorstep.

She would, of course, be staying in the area, said the inspector, and she echoed, 'Of course.'

James said, 'Her home address is the same as mine.'

Nobody showed any surprise at that but it had to be the clincher. She was not only James Halloran's friend, she was his live-in lady, which almost placed her above suspicion.

When they were out in the car again, she asked, 'Am I staying at your place?'

'You'd better, until this is over.'

'Thank you.' She wondered how it could ever be over. She said, 'I don't have an audition lined up.'

'Who's your agent?'

'Sandy Britton. Do you know her?'

'No, but I know several producers who should be hearing about you.'

Once that would have seemed the most exciting thing anyone could say to her, but today the stage was no longer the centre of her world, although she could feel the tears prickling again, the lump in her throat. 'You know something?' she said. 'In the garden, after the accident, when I was holding on to you it was like getting charged up, drawing strength. Rapport, they call that, don't they? Well, I'm doing it again now, feeling I'll be all right as long as I can reach out and grab you.'

'That was rapport, was it?' He seemed to be giving it some consideration, then suddenly he grinned wickedly. 'And I thought it was sex.'

That made her laugh, and her laughter did not turn into hysteria. It just lifted her spirits a little so that when they reached their next port-of-call, which was the theatre, she was slightly more able to cope.

One thing was plain. The news was out. There was a gaggle of Press in the car park racing towards the car, and as soon as Rosalyn opened her door somebody asked, 'Do you know where your brother is?'

Pictures were being taken before James could get round to her. 'No, I don't,' she said.

'How's Jeremy taking this?'

That was the local lad who had interviewed them both just after the accident and she shrieked, 'Why don't you ask him?' They would, of course, and that was where they would get their lurid quotes. She could just imagine what Hilary would have to say.

James had her arm and led her through the pack, heading for the stage door. 'We all understand our libel laws, don't we?' he said cheerfully, and now his smile was tigerish. 'So don't get carried away without counting the cost, because it could prove very expensive.'

Without him she would just have been running and begging, Leave me alone. She wouldn't have known what to say or do. She was still in shock, but she was taking her cues from James. 'I am all you've got,' he had said, and it was a near miracle that what she had got should be all that she needed.

She gave a Press interview in Kevin's office and she handled it well. When she faltered James took over, his personality dominating the proceedings so that harassment hardly entered into it, although had she been on her own they would probably have savaged her. She was so vulnerable that they would have considered it only doing their job it there had been a chance of getting away with it.

After the Press it was the company she had to face. By now they had all heard something of what had happened, and most of them seemed to have come along to the theatre to find out just what was going on.

The stage was crowded with actors, technicians, the production team, the cleaning staff, and when Kevin walked on with Rosalyn she felt she should be launching into her role, speaking words she had learned by heart.

As it happened, to her immense relief, she was immediately upstaged by James. Dealing with professional scandalmongers at the Press conference he had been steely and dangerous, but here he was a different man. He knew none of them, but he stood with a protective arm around Rosalyn, speaking as if he was among friends.

In a way she supposed he was. They were her friends and he was her champion, but she would not have been taking their support for granted as he seemed to do. They had heard about the robbery, he said, and they would realise that Rosalyn was more shocked than any of them.

Heaven knew she was. The way she was feeling she must look dreadful, and their sympathetic reaction was immediate. There was pity for her in every face, and she turned her head into James's shoulder as he went on, so bluntly that most of them gasped, 'You'll also have heard that Ben can't be contacted. By now he could have turned up—there's no law that says a man must never leave his home—but meanwhile Rosalyn needs her friends if it's only to keep away the gutter Press.'

She raised her head to look at him gratefully. She didn't have to face them cold; he had broken the ice, and they were gathering around her, petting her, hugging her, saying, 'What a carry-on'.

Behind her back they would still decide that Ben's decamping was too much of a coincidence for someone with a clear conscience, but James Halloran seemed like a man whose judgement you could trust and he had no doubts about Rosalyn. He knew, and they all knew, that Rosalyn would be going through hell because this was a nasty business. But she was straight as they came and she would never have had anything to do with that break-in at the Hiatts'.

It was a vote of confidence as they rallied round, and when James said, 'I have to go; will you come with me?' she was able to tell him,

'I'll be all right. But you will come back and sit through the play? I might get booed tonight.'

He grinned. 'Take it for appreciation—you are playing a killer. I'll be here and then we'll go home.' He kissed her lightly, and for a moment she clung to him, longing to keep him here or to go with him. But he had other calls and he had done her proud; she had to start showing some spirit.

The break-in was hot gossip, of course, but Rosalyn would hardly be wanting to talk about that. And the girls at least were more interested in what was going on between her and James Halloran than what had happened to a few old paintings.

'When he said "we'll go home",' probed Lou, 'where exactly did he mean?'

'His apartment,' said Rosalyn. 'I'm moving in.' And it was the last thing she had expected. That there could be a time today when almost every woman around would have changed places with her.

Even in his absence James was a shield. The Press remembered that he was her lawyer, her friends rallied round, and knowing that he was coming back for her helped her to get through the hours until she would see him again.

When the coast seemed clear she managed to slip out of the theatre and drive away with Margie. They went far enough for Rosalyn not to be recognised, walked over the moorland acres of a National Trust park, and ate in a snack bar.

Margie had declared fervently at once that she was sure Rosalyn's brother had nothing to do with anything, and that was all that was said on the matter. It was never out of their minds but for now the problem was ignored, and Rosalyn was smuggled back into the theatre just in time to get changed for tonight's performance.

James was already backstage, and just seeing him lifted her mood from gloom to elation. As he came to meet her she asked, 'Anything happened?'

'Not a thing.' Which meant that Ben was still on the run.

'Margie and I had a nice relaxing time, away from it all,' she said brightly. 'Now I guess the fun starts.'

'We can only hope so.' His deep voice gave such a sexy drawl that she laughed, wrinkling her nose.

'Yes, please,' she said, and slipped her hand through his arm to walk along the corridor to the dressing-room.

In her heart she knew that Ben was almost certainly involved and that she would suffer for him because she loved him. But James was a rock and he was here for her now—so long as he stayed with her she could face the future.

There was hardly anyone in the audience who would not have heard about the art robbery and Rosalyn's link with the Hiatts. Not everyone was wised up yet about her brother's part in this, but Rosalyn was still the focus of avid curiosity.

She could sense the stares and the whispers as she made her moves and spoke her lines. It was a full house. James was siting in the stalls, and when the bursts of applause came it seemed to her they started with him, that he was making them accept and applaud her. She knew for sure that every time she looked at him she found the strength she needed to deliver a glittering performance.

At the end they clapped heartily and by then James was waiting in the wings, getting her away almost faster than the last time. She didn't even stay to change. She grabbed her clothes and purse, dived into the car and kept her head down, hardly daring to look up even when they reached the parking bay.

She just wanted to get inside the apartment and have his arms around her, and she scuttled into the lift, looking nowhere but straight ahead.

She was breathing fast when he opened the door. 'I'll be right back,' he said.

'Where are you going?'

'Just making sure we won't be disturbed. A word with Joe. We need space and peace. We have plans to work out.' He stroked her hair with a tender touch. 'Things to do,' he said.

They had things to do that she had never experienced even in dreams. 'Come back soon.' If you are more than five minutes away I could pass out from wanting you.

And plans to make that had nothing to do with dreams but everything to do with the nightmare that Ben had unleashed. Where was Ben? He had said that wherever he went he would keep in touch with her and she thought that she believed him.

He might have phoned already. He could have rung the flat and disguised his voice and whoever took a call might have forgotten to tell her. She had been in a mad rush before the curtain had gone up.

Lou or Roddy could have given Ben this number— Rosalyn had scribbled it on that envelope. Ben might have rung and left a message on this answering machine.

She went into the study and switched on. If James came in it would be awkward but she wouldn't really listen to his business and personal calls. Nor did she, because almost at once a husky voice was whispering, 'Hello, darling, it's Mariella. I'll be with you tomorrow—I'm coming home.'

CHAPTER EIGHT

ROSALYN turned off the voice, pressed down to rewind, and backed out of the room, eyes on the answerphone as if it were a cobra poised to strike.

When James walked into the apartment she faced him with a smile. 'May I clean up and change?' She was still in stage make-up, wearing a shimmery silver dress.

'Of course.' He indicated the bathroom. She took her jeans and shirt in with her, and once the door was closed she stopped smiling and chewed hard on her underlip.

Whoever Mariella was her timing was good. Tonight of all nights, when they really needed to be alone. James had gone to see a man who presumably could hold off intruders, but Mariella had beaten him to it. She was here already. James could be listening to her husky voice right now.

Anyone could start with, 'Hello, darling.' That made her nothing special. But the way she said, 'I'll be with you tomorrow—I'm coming home,' was much more intimate. Alarm bells were ringing for Rosalyn, telling her that Mariella was the rival in James's past, and she was staggered by the ferocity of her own reaction to that. It was a savage determination to fight with no holds barred.

Mariella would be with James tomorrow, and tomorrow was nearly here. Well, she couldn't have him. Rosalyn would still be needing him, and not just as a shield against the slings and arrows of life, but because he was suddenly the one who mattered most in her life.

Because of that she would need him and want him, now and forever. And maybe Mariella's timing had not been so brilliant, after all, because it still left Rosalyn with tonight, and tonight she would do anything that would keep James for her alone and for no other woman.

Although she could surely have done without this. Ben was trouble enough—they had to talk about Ben—and even if James never mentioned her Mariella's little time bomb was ticking away over there in the answerphone.

I wish we could leave them all behind, she thought fervently. I'd like James to take me somewhere secret and safe, like a desert island or the moon, just for tonight. Well, I don't think I'd mind if it was for the rest of our lives but I would be thankful just for tonight.

She found a bottle of cleansing lotion in a cabinet, slipped the narrow straps of her dress off her shoulders, poured lotion on to cotton wool and was beginning to dab her face with it when there was a tap on the door and she looked out.

'I've been listening to the callers,' he told her, 'and there are several I can't see Joe managing to hold off. We might be better out of here.'

'Right with you.' Frantically she grabbed a white bath towel and rubbed her face, transferring a mess of greasepaint, yanked up her shoulder-straps and rolled her clothes and purse into a tight bundle.

He smiled at her haste. 'You've got time to change. It isn't exactly a bomb alert.'

Funny you should say that, she thought; that's exactly how I would have described Mariella. 'Let's go,' she begged.

A door on the landing led to a service staircase. As they went down, she said, 'Suppose they're waiting out there?'

She and her brother were spicy copy. Reporters and photographers could pop up anywhere, although they probably had enough for the morning papers.

'Think positive,' said James.

She answered, 'Most of the time I do. But I've had a few shocks lately and my nerves aren't as steady as they used to be.'

At the bottom of the stairs he took her in his arms and she put a hand on his shoulder and rested against his long hard body. She could feel the stirring in her flesh, the singing in her blood, as for a moment she pressed closer and he held her tighter.

'They call it rapport,' he said, and she laughed.

'And here's me thinking it was good old sex.'

'That, too,' he said. 'If there should be anyone hanging around out there we may have to take the car to get rid of them. Otherwise it's straight across to the towpath.'

Her shoes were low-heeled pumps. She could have run in them if she'd had to, but the flagstoned area behind the building was empty and they crossed quickly to the high wooden gate in the red-brick wall.

She had often walked by the river, and fed the ducks and the swans, but never at night. As late as this pale moonlight turned the river into a broad silver road, and the alders and willows into dark impenetrable shadows.

'Where are we going?' she asked.

'I've got a boat moored just along here.'

'So's Jeremy. The *Nereid*.'

'That's the one. Jeremy uses her. So do a number of my friends.'

The last time Rosalyn had been here was with Jeremy, on their way to spend the day on his boat. Well, he might not have actually said he owned the boat. She couldn't remember and it didn't matter, but she remembered the carefree fun of it all.

That seemed as if it had been another life where everything was on the surface and nothing struck at her heart. She had believed she was happy. Now she was half out of her mind, worrying about Ben, but she was also passionately alive for the very first time.

This man beside her had shown her what happiness could mean, and how loving would be; having him with her seemed to outweigh her misery, but she had to ask, 'Did any of the messages sound like Ben?'

'No. But Charles is home. I spoke to him earlier from the office and he rang to say he'd arrived next door. We could bank on his turning up. Were you up to seeing Charles?'

'No, *no*. Is Hilary back too?' She dreaded facing them again. They had been so kind to her, and look how she had repaid them.

'Hilary is having a mini-breakdown in Wales,' said James, and she could have wept.

'Isn't it *horrible*.'

He agreed, 'It's appalling. But none of the blame is yours.'

The night seemed to be full of sighs, the river lapping against the banks, a breeze stirring the trees. She sighed too, facing what everybody knew. 'Ben could be involved. If he is I more or less let them in, didn't I?'

'No, you did not.'

'Well, I surely didn't mean to.'

'So let's change the subject,' he said briskly, and she took a deep breath and forced brightness into her voice.

'How long have you had the *Nereid*? She's a super boat.'

'I bought her last year from a man who'd just married, then found his wife got seasick on a canal so a boat wasn't much use to them.'

'What rotten luck.' She sighed again, fooling this time. 'The trouble some men have with their women.'

'So they tell me,' he said. 'Passes belief, doesn't it, Becky? Why they put up with it I do not know.'

She had been trouble from the start, but he liked her enough to shoulder her troubles. Maybe he even loved her a little. Maybe after tonight he would love her more.

She said softly, 'I wouldn't know either.' He took her little bundle of clothes and she put a hand through his arm. 'This is nice,' she said. 'Strolling down the river. What do we do if someone has sailed off with the *Nereid*

'Call on friends.'

There were houses now, standing back from river frontages, but nobody in the gardens. A riverside pub threw lights across a lawn reaching the towpath, but the tables were cleared, the chairs neatly stacked. A barge had lighted windows and voices reached them as they passed by, but the moored boats were mostly shuttered and silent, and after ten minutes of fairly brisk walking they arrived at the *Nereid*.

Even the boat looked different at night. She remembered it as being smaller and brighter in the sunshine. Jeremy had joked when he ceremoniously handed her on deck, 'Once aboard the lugger and the girl is mine,' and she had laughed too, saying,

'Sorry, but somehow I can't see you as a pirate.'

James, now, would have made a suave and sinister buccaneer, and on or off the lugger the girl *was* his, because when Jeremy put his arms around her she hardly felt a thing, but when James held her every nerve in her body leapt into fevered life.

She asked, 'Are we staying here?' It was a private mooring with a landing-stage; she remembered the house beyond the trees.

But he said, 'We'll go as far as the island.'

She knew where he meant. Mid-river and before the lock there was a small island, a bird sanctuary, and when they moored again it was in a tiny sheltered bay where nobody was likely to find them and where the little saloon, with its gleaming wood panelling and mellow wall-lights, was a haven.

On the *Nereid* with Jeremy she had rushed around, looking at everything, wanting to cook something in the tiny compact kitchen, to take over the wheel and try her hand at steering, playing games like a child on holiday. Jeremy had been a playmate, but now she was here with James all she wanted to do was go to bed with him.

He had dropped her bundle of clothing on the wide settee that ran the length of the saloon and he was opening cupboards in the galley. She loved the breadth of his shoulders and the smooth stuff of his jacket. She had never met anyone before whom she ached to touch, but it was true what she had told him, 'I feel I'll be all right as long as I can reach out and grab you.'

Right now her fingertips were tingling and she pressed them to her lips. The silver lamé dress was stiff-bodiced and tight-waisted with a side-split skirt, designed to shine on stage, and she was beginning to feel slightly ridiculous in it.

She said, 'I'll get into something more comfortable,' and he turned. 'Well,' she babbled, 'this is wardrobe department property; I'd better keep it in good nick.'

When he grinned she pulled a laughing face. She was not suggesting he was likely to rip it off her, worse luck. 'Anyhow, it scratches,' she said.

'Then by all menas take it off.'

Not out here. She went into the cabin with the double bunk. A theatrical creation, velcro-taped and safety-pinned, this was not the easiest dress to get out of. Wriggling free could have been more of a comic turn than a turn on. Besides, stripping nearly naked in front of a man who hadn't even loosened his tie yet was hardly a natural approach to lovemaking.

Not that that really mattered, but she hoped he would follow her into the cabin, and she got out of her 'killer costume' and peered into a mirror backing a small table, seeing what should have been no surprise but still came as a shock, that she had never looked less seductive.

She was a *mess*! Make-up smeared, hair backcombed into a wild halo, bruising from the car accident fading but only to a paler green. I could be from outer space, she thought, but even a Martian wouldn't fancy me, so how the hell do I imagine I am going to upstage Mariella?

She pulled on her shirt, which covered the bruises. Underneath that there was nothing wrong with her figure. She tissued away more of the greasepaint residue, and dragged a comb fiercely and painfully through her tousled hair. And then James opened the door to ask, 'Are you all right?'

She must have looked better than she had five minutes ago, but probably more woebegone, her eyes swimming with tears from the last yank that had left her comb stuck in a tangle.

'Fine,' she said, with spurious gaiety. 'But I've just seen myself in that glass and I don't seem to be wearing well.'

'It's been a rough day.'

'It hasn't aged you.'

No long hard day was going to get him down. He was strong and tough and handsome, and her bones liquefied as she looked at him so that she drooped, her hands dropping into her lap, her comb left in her hair.

'It hasn't aged you,' he said. 'You look about ten years old.'

That was not what she wanted. She wanted to be all woman and the sexiest siren since Cleopatra. 'So tell me a bedtime story,' she said.

'Come here.' She got off the bunk and took the two paces that brought her up against him, and once there she closed her eyes and went where he took her. On the long settee beside him she opened her eyes. Squirming slightly around and lifting her feet up, she was almost lying down, so that she could smile up at him, and he took that stupid comb out and combed her hair smoothly and soothingly.

She could feel the tangled knots falling free, her whole body relaxing right down to her feet, and she wriggled her toes in drowsy ecstasy. This was lovely. She never wanted the stroking to stop. There was no need to say anything and her voice was hardly more than a whisper, but the words came. 'You do think Ben's in it?'

'Over his head.' His fingers brushed her temples.

'What—will happen to him?'

'He could make a getaway. He could get caught. Odds in the long run on the latter.'

'You can't win 'em all,' Ben had said, and this had been a loser from the start. . .

'Do you mind if I tell you about him?' she asked.

He went on stroking her hair. 'No, I don't mind.' Her first memories were bearable because her brother had been with her, and she talked about their early days, when Ben had protected her. Because he always had, as best he could. When they were parted Aunt Eleanor had taken her and the orphanage had taken him, but Ben had found her again at a time when she'd really needed him.

He had looked after her again, helped her again. Now if he was in trouble it might be of his own making, but he was still her brother, all the family she had.

She talked slowly, pausing, sometimes stumbling, telling herself and James her reasons for believing that he cared about her; he always had.

He always had been there for her, except for the time when they had lost touch before Aunt Eleanor died. She had not been able to reach him then and that was how it was again. Tonight Ben could be the other side of the world for all she knew. She could have been alone tonight in spite of her friends and her fans.

James had not spoken. Nor did he now. But he had stroked her hair as she talked and the caress seemed like a promise that she need never be alone while she could creep into his arms.

She looked into the dark eyes and saw tenderness in them. The hard mouth was close to her lips and a surge of longing arched her back, pushing her up against him. 'Will you make love to me?' she whispered, and he kissed her lightly and promised,

'I'll make it right for you.'

For a little while he held her in silence as she clung to him. Then he carried her, limp as a sleeper, into the cabin, and lowered her gently on to the bunk.

She pulled her shirt over her head, unclasped her bra and slipped out of her briefs. Then she watched him as he stripped and the long lean athlete's body was how she had known it would be. Magnificent. When he stood looking down at her she held out her arms.

Then again she was in his arms and the relief was indescribable. He *could* make things right. All that she had to do was let go in every way, thinking of nothing, floating free.

'Love me,' she murmured, and slowly and sensuously, caressing her inch by throbbing inch, he took her over the threshold of any pleasure she had ever known until she was moaning and writhing with exquisite sensations.

It was like hearing music when you had been deaf all your life, like flowers opening in slow motion. She could smell perfume, feel her own deep, warm, pulsating contractions as he moved with deliberate slowness inside her.

Nothing else mattered while this was happening to her. All fear and all pain were forgotten. She was drowning in rapture, drifting into sleep, comforted and pleasured by a consummately skilful lover.

She shuddered with pleasure again as she began to wake, stretching slowly, yawning and smiling under the coolness of a cotton sheet. Her eyelids felt too heavy to lift and the same sweet languor weighed down her limbs. She wanted to lie here, luxuriating, feeling beautiful and cherished because that was what she had been.

James had cherished her and it had been marvellous, and she must have slept for quite a while because he was no longer in this bunk of a bed. She opened her eyes wide enough then, checking on that in the shadowy dark, and elbowed herself upright because he was not in the cabin either.

She listened and she could hear the soft splashing of water against the boat but no other sound. The door was not closed but no light came from the saloon, although of course he was somewhere aboard, and she reached to pull the curtain from across the porthole, letting moonlight in.

Suddenly she was fully awake, as if dawn were breaking and the morning cold. She sat, chin on her knees and her hands clasped round her ankles, not shivering but feeling the slightest of chills on her warm skin as her mind cleared.

If James had been within reach everything would have been easy, but for the moment she was alone, and that was time enough to start wondering if she ever had touched him beneath the surface. The lovemaking had been like an incredibly sensuous dream; her pleasure was mind-blowing, and that was because of his skill and control.

Trying to remember a dream usually ended in most of it fading beyond recall, but, reliving this dream and her own abandonment, she was conscious of what must have been his restraint.

It had been his pleasure too, she was sure of that, but at no stage had he been transported out of this world or out of his mind. He had always been in command, of himself and of her. While she had slept, drugged with delight, he must have lain beside her for a while. Maybe he was physically relaxed and satisfied, but he had other things on his mind besides her. Mariella, maybe, who would be with him very soon

She reached down to scoop up her shirt from the floor and pulled it over her head, then wriggled into her briefs. She was wasting no more time sleeping, not alone she wasn't. She was finding James.

She didn't find him at once. She tugged a light-switch cord but below deck seemed to be empty and she went up the little flight of steps into the open air. He was on the foredeck and the light had warned him she was coming so that he had turned towards her. Dawn was not breaking yet. There were thick clusters of stars in the sky and the moon was riding high.

She smiled and it seemed an actressy thing to do, holding the smile and walking slowly when she wanted to run and grab him and gabble, I woke and you'd gone and I don't ever want that to happen because what can I do without you?

A splinter from the deck boards pricked her toe but she didn't look down and she kept smiling. When she reached him she went into his arms and said, 'What are you doing? Communing with nature?

'Something like that.' He was shirtless and she laid her cheek against the taut rippling muscles of his chest.

'I woke and you'd gone,' she said.

'Not far. If you'd called I'd have heard you.'

She had been scared, not that he had really gone of course—he'd hardly have swum to the river-bank—but that he was moving away from her. Now he was saying call and I'll come to you, and it was nice to be told that even if it was a promise he might not always be able to keep.

A chilly little breeze was blowing over the water, prickling goose-flesh on her bare arms and legs, and she wondered if he had been thinking of Mariella out here. Where 'home' was—if it was James's apartment. If Mariella turned up there she was going to find Rosalyn as a sitting tenant in the guest-room. Or maybe Mariella would be expecting to share the master bedroom.

Rosalyn shivered, and James said, 'It's cold up here. Let's get below.'

In the galley he uncorked a bottle. 'I found this in a cupboard.'

'What is it?' It was a bottle of wine, anyone could see that, but he brought out two plastic tumblers with it, poured a little, tasted it and said,

'Lord knows. Furniture polish?'

She sipped from her glass. 'No, it isn't. It's quite a pleasant plonk.' She took another swallow. 'Well, I like it.'

'Good,' he said, and she thought it could have been left over from the picnic afloat which she had shared with Jeremy. She remembered that there was tinned and packaged food in the galley, and they had brought wine and fruit with them, but she could hardly remember Jeremy. The man lounging beside her had taken such vivid possession of her senses that his was the only face she could see or recall.

Bare-chested, barefoot, he exuded male sensuality, and she wanted him again, she wanted him *now*. She could be greedy with him, downright voracious, but she shouldn't be showing it too blatantly, and she lifted the tumbler to her lips, then raised it and, for something to say, toasted, 'Absent friends.'

'Wherever they are,' he said.

She wondered if he was thinking of Mariella; he probably thought she was thinking of Ben. She hadn't meant anyone in particular—it was a cliché—but now she asked, 'You—wouldn't help him?' and that was asking for what she got. A flat rejection.

'Frankly, I don't give a damn what happens to him.'

Why should anyone else give a damn? and she wished she could stop caring herself. 'I do,' she said miserably. 'I suppose I always will. You said you were prejudiced against him from the beginning because of the fire, but that was me too. I was his alibi. If you think it was fraud for him it was fraud for me.'

'You were seventeen. He was years older, vastly more experienced. At that stage he might have been expected to have undue influence on you.'

When she was seventeen Ben could do no wrong in her eyes. Since then she had become older and wiser, but he had never risked asking her to lie for him.

She put her tumbler aside, slowly and carefully as if it were over-full and could be spilled. She didn't look back at James, and her voice was flat. 'I thought he was telling the truth, that he was in all night. I'm usually a light sleeper—I wake easily. I was so sure and I was so angry that anyone could suspect him. I remember that claims inspector who kept questioning me——' James's friend who had discussed it with him all those years ago '—He was Ben's enemy and I hated him.'

'And now?'

She was still turned away, the dull hopelessness was still in her voice. 'It doesn't matter any more, but yes, I suppose I could have taken sleeping pills. He could have gone out. A lot of things could have happened that I wouldn't even let myself consider then. I don't know if it was a set-up job but if it was he took a gamble on me.'

'I think he did,' James said grimly. 'And he had to know what this break-in might do to you.'

She shrank a little, huddling into herself, and he said as if she had spoken, 'It won't harm you, I promise you that, but if and when he surfaces he'll hardly be expecting me to represent him.' He put steadying hands each side of her anxious face so that she had to look up at him. 'He'll survive, sweetheart. I can see him doing time philosophically and coming out in fine fettle.'

'You can't win 'em all.' He had had a jaunty resignation when he'd said it. . . She sighed, 'You think he's a dead loss, don't you?'

James said drily, 'Not entirely. He has his points. He's fond of you. He's proud of you. He even looks like you in a poor light. But he's causing my friends great distress, and, unless the pictures are recovered, the kind of loss that no insurance can make up for, and right now I could murder the little bastard.'

Me too, she thought, much as I love him. Of course James couldn't and wouldn't help Ben, although Ben had sent her to plead for him. 'Offer him anything,' Ben had said, and a sudden blush scalded her because what had just happened between herself and James might seem the sort of thing Ben had had in mind.

She glanced towards the cabin door, only her eyes moving, the rest of her still, and stammered, 'You didn't think—that was for Ben?'

He shook his head, 'No. Because of Ben maybe. Because you needed a comfort blanket.'

She had been marvellously consoled and the burning blush became a glow. 'Thank you,' she said, and he raised her hand to his lips and kissed it. 'I'm sorry I let you down when you asked me.' The raised eyebrow queried that. 'On our way back from Heritage Halt when we were talking about love, pleasure and pain, and you said pain would be remembered. You were remembering, weren't you?'

That surprised him. 'That was very perceptive of you.'

'Was she another Becky? Was she why you didn't trust women who carried on like Becky Sharp?'

'You don't want to hear this.'

'Fair's fair; you seem to know everything that ever happened to me.'

'Well, her name's Mariella.' She was clairvoyant. Never before and probably never again, but she had *known* it was Mariella. 'And all this was a long time ago.' It might have begun in the past but darling Mariella was arriving today and you couldn't get more up-to-the-minute than that.

She settled herself in the crook of his arm, as if she was preparing for a bedtime story that she was no longer sure she wanted to hear. 'Was she beautiful?' she asked lightly.

'Incredibly,' and already jealousy was tearing her apart. 'We were students. She was taking art.'

Pictures unfolded in her mind. James—even before that aura of power he'd acquired with the years—and a ravishing girl must have made a sensational couple. They must have stopped the traffic. And the deep drawling voice would always thrill her, even when he was talking about another woman and saying, 'We planned to marry,' with all that must have meant burning in her brain. 'Until I took her home to meet my uncle. He was rich and I had damn all and she married him.'

How horrific that would be! 'How awful,' she gasped. 'What——?'

'End of story,' he said. It wasn't, of course, or Mariella would not have left that message. 'The moral being; charmers can be schemers, and she did come to mind when we were talking. It dawned on me then that ours could be a very different relationship.'

He might mean in the shallows where there was no risk of pain, but she was in dangerously deep waters whether he was or not. She took a good slug of Jeremy's plonk and said wistfully, 'Different from any I've ever come across,' and laughed a little because he was here, wasn't he? They were together.

'What's the joke?' He smiled at her and she smiled back.

'Very elegant trousers, but they don't exactly go with bare feet.'

'What's wrong with my feet?'

Long feet on very long legs, they looked as well constructed as the rest of him and she said, 'As feet go they seem in splendid order.'

She remembered stepping on the splinter on deck and twisted her foot to check, but there was no sign of damage, only a slightly grubby sole, and she put her feet together, holding them up for inspection. Her nails were pearly pink and she asked, 'How do you like mine?'

'Charming.'

'They are, aren't they?' She drained her tumbler and poured herself a little more. 'Would you like me to give you a foot massage?'

'Is that one of your talents?'

'Could be; I've never tried before. Or how about me running up and down your spine? I've seen that done on telly. Or was it in the *Kama Sutra*?'

'Fascinating. But I'd rather you got some practice in before you start dancing on my spine.'

'Right,' she said. 'Now who do I know who wouldn't mind being trampled on?'

She remembered Jeremy then and reached for James, and along his shoulder-blade her fingertips felt scar tissue. There was a long raised line in the smooth brown skin of his back and she asked, 'What happened?'

'What? Oh, I fell off a motor bike twenty-odd years ago.'

'Not a battle scar?' She put her lips to his shoulder. 'Only that first ride you took me on, when you were going to feed me and warn me off Jeremy, I thought, He could have battle scars. I never thought I'd get the chance to check.'

When he laughed, she said, 'I don't suppose you were wondering what I looked like under my clothes. Well, I was showing a fair amount in the dressing-room and I know what you were thinking about me.'

'I was thinking,' he said, 'We've got a right one here.'

'When did you change your mind?'

'I haven't.' The dark eyes looked straight into hers. 'I think I might well have *the* right one.' He was not smiling now and she whispered,

'You'll remember me, won't you? You're good for me. Nothing seems too bad when I'm with you.'

He ran a finger slowly round her face, tracing the contours of her jaw, sending her heartbeats racing. 'I'd put it stronger than that,' he said. 'I'd say that when I'm with you everything is absolutely right. You're wild and sweet and very beautiful and I could be dead and dust and still be remembering you.'

She had never thought she would ever hear him say anything like that. She gasped, her mouth falling open, and she heard herself croak, 'But I've been nothing but trouble.'

His fingers reached the softness of her throat where a pulse was leaping like mad. 'You can't believe that,' he said.

'Well, most of the time.'

'Well, I wouldn't have missed a minute of it.' Fountains of delight rose in her, making her blink as if champagne bubbles were tickling her nose. 'So just go on needing me,' he said.

'Oh, I *will*.' There was no way she could stop needing him, when she was starving for him with only one reason. 'I love you,' she said.

'Thank God for that.' And she prayed while she asked, 'Do you love me?'

'Totally. You are the loveliest thing that's ever happened to me.' And it seemed to her then that she would never pray for anything else as long as she lived; she would just go on giving thanks.

She was nestling so closely against him that she could hear his heart beating with hers, making strange deep music. She listened to the heartbeats through the dark hairs on his chest and the taste of him was on her lips. She had not known she needed anyone until he came, but now she couldn't imagine life without him. Touching and tasting, she was still begging, 'Hold me.'

He held her and told her, 'I'll never let you go,' and she looked up, her eyes searching his.

She said. 'The last time I gave you nothing.'

'You let me comfort you.'

She had seen the tenderness in his eyes before but now she saw more love than she had ever imagined, and she said, 'This time will you make love with me?'

'Always,' he said, and they went smiling into the cabin, and lay down facing each other. Then he kissed her mouth, his tongue between her parted lips speaking a silent and secret language. He could devour me, she thought, and I would still be under his skin, the beat of his heart.

For both it was a journey of joy, giving and taking, slowly and sensually reaching the point of no return together, soaring to the heights of intensity in a violent rhythm, until fulfilment erupted with such piercing sweetness that she screamed his name. Because he had brought her to her kingdom but she would never find it again without him.

Her fingers were caught in his hair and his arms were locked around her, and when she slept this time she woke to find him still with her.

Dawn had broken. Daylight was streaming through the porthole, and James lay beside her looking down at her. When she reached up to touch his cheek she could feel roughness, following the dark shadow of a beard, and she said, 'A week without a razor and you'd make a splendid pirate.'

'We'll try it some time.'

'That will be lovely.' She sat up and looked at herself, 'I shouldn't be getting personal about appearances. Me with my bruises. Pea-green isn't a pretty skin colour. Didn't you notice them?'

'The first time, yes,' he said. 'The second, I'm afraid not.'

The seat-belt bruises more or less ran diagonally across her shoulder and breast, and there was discolouration on her waist and upper arms; she said, 'I'm a sort of map of the islands.'

'So you are.' He trailed a light tickling fingertip. 'The twelve islands: Rhodes, Symi, and so on.'

'How about this?' She peered over her shoulder.

'Isle of Wight?'

'Maybe. And on my back?'

'Paler here. Vanishing under the waves. Atlantis.'

With her back turned to him she said, very casually, 'About Mariella.'

'What about her?'

'What happened afterwards?'

'She became a rich widow. In a few years she had the estate and the old family home.'

'And?'

'She sold out, which she was legally entitled to do. She bought a home here and another in Florida.

'Did you keep in touch?'

His voice was cynically amused. 'As my prospects improved.'

'Were you—lovers again?'

'No.'

She was so glad to hear that but she still asked, 'You still see her?'

'Occasionally. She's arriving at Heathrow today, as you very well know.'

She swivelled round then to face him, wide-eyed with innocence. 'What makes you think, I know?' and he laughed.

'Because I know you Becky. You heard her on the answerphone, didn't you?'

She didn't deny it because all her acting skill couldn't fool him. She would never be able to keep anything from him and she would never want to. 'Well—yes,' she said, and, a little apprehensively, 'Are you sure you like Becky?'

'I've learned to appreciate her.' He drew her down beside him. 'Every tantrum. Every island.' He kissed her shoulder and breast and his lips sent tremors through her. 'To the stage where I am besotted with her. The trouble with the original Becky was that she never met her match.'

'You don't mean her master?'

'Certainly not. Becky was never for taming.' He put an arm over her, pinning her down. 'But while I've got you here, in what I hope is a co-operative mood, will you marry me?'

His voice was steady but she felt him tremble, and

she couldn't speak and he said, 'Whether you do or not you'll never be free of me, but I would enjoy saying "my wife".'

She thought, I would love to say 'my husband'. She said, 'For better or worse you're lumbered with me but yes, please, I would very much like to marry you.'

It was quite a while before she remembered what might be called an impediment. James was dressing and she was considering getting up and dressed herself when she remembered Ben. That got her head off the pillow. She had been watching James, still hardly believing her luck because he was so stunning in every way, but now she asked jerkily, 'How about my brother? How about him as your brother?'

He opened a drawer, took out a towel and said, 'Every family should have a black sheep. Mariella is a fairly distant relation and nuisance value is all we can count on her for, so Ben will have to be our black sheep.'

'I do love you,' she said.

'That's a good start to the day.' His smile would always turn her on and he said, 'Do stop smiling like that or I won't be able to keep my hands off you. Now, tea or coffee?'

'I'll come.'

She swung her legs to get off the bunk but he said, 'I'll bring it. Lie there and get your strength up. It's going to be another tough day. But it will have its highlights.' He came across and she flung her arms around his neck.'

'Will it not?' she said, because this was the first day of the rest of their lives. Together.

Next month's Romances

Each month, you can choose from a world of variety in romance with Mills & Boon. These are the new titles to look out for next month.

TEMPESTUOUS REUNION Lynne Graham

A CURE FOR LOVE Penny Jordan

UNDERCOVER AFFAIR Lilian Peake

GHOST OF THE PAST Sally Wentworth

ISTANBUL AFFAIR Joanna Mansell

ROARKE'S KINGDOM Sandra Marton

WHEN LOVE RETURNS Vanessa Grant

DANGEROUS INFATUATION Stephanie Howard

LETHAL ATTRACTION Rebecca King

STORMY RELATIONSHIP Margaret Mayo

HONG KONG HONEYMOON Lee Wilkinson

CONTRACT TO LOVE Kate Proctor

WINTER DESTINY Grace Green

AFRICAN ASSIGNMENT Carol Gregor

THE CHALK LINE Kate Walker

STARSIGN

HUNTED HEART Kristy McCallum

Available from Boots, Martins, John Menzies, W.H. Smith and other paperback stockists.

Also available from Mills and Boon Reader Service, P.O. Box 236, Thornton Road, Croydon, Surrey CR9 3RU.